A MOMENT'S PASSION . . .

Skye, the granddaughter of a Scottish lord, and Hector, a grounds-keeper's son, stood on the grassy moor. He refused to consider himself her equal. Their anger hung between them.

"Do you want me to go?" she asked.

"Is it likely that I should want that?" he asked hoarsely. Their eyes met. Slowly Hector raised his arms and drew Skye to him. He felt the softness of her mouth beneath his.

"I love . . . you," she said tremulously.

"Oh, my God!" Hector whispered. "What have I done?"

BROKEN
BARRIERS

Barbara Cartland

PYRAMID BOOKS  NEW YORK

BROKEN BARRIERS
A PYRAMID BOOK

Pyramid edition published September 1976

Printed in the United States of America

Pyramid Books are published by Pyramid Publications (Harcourt Brace Jovanovich, Inc.). Its trademarks, consisting of the word "Pyramid" and the portrayal of a pyramid, are registered in the United States Patent Office.

PYRAMID PUBLICATIONS (Harcourt Brace Jovanovich, Inc.).
757 Third Avenue, New York, N.Y. 10017

AUTHOR'S NOTE

I wrote this novel in 1938 when my brother was the Member of Parliament for the Kings Norton version of Birmingham.

His constituency included the Austin works. Sir Herbert Austin had started work by repairing bicycles.

The enormous difficulties between the social classes were very great in those days, but a millionaire tycoon moved in a world of his own.

In a year's time the War was to sweep away many businesses and many centuries-old social values.

Broken
Barriers

CHAPTER ONE

1938

Norman Melton sat at his desk, fingering the pages of the contract that lay before him awaiting his signature.

Abruptly, without looking up, he said:

"Well, we have pulled it off, Johnson."

"Yes, Sir Norman."

"You have read this, I suppose?"

"Yes, Sir Norman."

"You have made all those corrections that were agreed with Miller?"

"Yes, Sir Norman."

He picked up his pen.

"This should be marked as a red-letter day on our almanacs. It's the best deal the Melton Motor Company has ever done or is ever likely to do."

"Yes, Sir Norman."

Sir Norman put down his pen with a gesture of exasperation.

"Damn you, Johnson! Can't you ever say anything but yes? Send Miller to me. No, wait, I will ring when I want him."

Johnson, an aggrieved expression on his face, left the room.

Alone, Sir Norman rose to his feet and moved towards the window. He felt nervy and wondered vaguely to himself why Johnson's usual monosyllabic manner annoyed him so much today.

He was used to curbing his impatience before his subordinates. He remembered vividly the years when he himself hated the blustering of his superiors.

Johnson, for all his efficiency, was the type of secretary he disliked. He was deemed indispensable, yet the man's lack of individuality and personality made his employer long to startle him out of his conventional attitude.

'I need a holiday,' Sir Norman told himself, looking out on to the busy yard below his office window.

The siren had just gone for lunch and the men were streaming out of the workshops, struggling into their coats as they did so, taking packets of sandwiches from the pockets or lighting with relief a cigarette after the long hours of abstinence.

High above the buildings was the great sign 'The Melton Motor Company'.

The yard was four stories below him and Sir Norman, watching, felt for a moment as if he, Director and Chairman of this vast factory, was also the controller of the destiny of each man who worked for him.

'I am a part of them, one of them,' Sir Norman tried to tell himself.

But he knew that it was a false illusion. He had grown away from them and was changed now as completely from the men who had once been his comrades as he was removed from the life they lived and the work they did.

He was the boss.

He remembered his own feelings when as a young man he had come into the factory—a small, gloomy building it had been then—and he had first seen the heavy-moustached, black-coated figure of Edward Buller.

He had little thought then that twenty-nine years later he would be in Buller's place and that the works would bear his name as the outward sign of his success.

Today was the greatest triumph of all.

He had hardly dared to believe that he would land for his own firm the Government contract for a 'shadow' factory, but he had accomplished it.

Once the contract waiting on his desk was signed, the orders would go out for new buildings, new machinery, and for at least five thousand more workers. It was a triumph for which he had been working for nearly three months.

His factory was small compared to the other great firms who were bearing their part in the rearmament programme.

There were a dozen other factories of the same size all over the country. There was no reason why the Melton Motor Company should have been chosen except that its

10

director had the drive, the originality, and the vision which were required if the work undertaken was to be successful.

The Melton Motor Company had been sensationally successful over the last five years.

The shares had risen until the shareholders' meetings were nothing but a celebration of renewed confidence, congratulations and good wishes.

But the Chairman, on his forty-second birthday, had waked to the fact that he had joined the ranks of bored millionaires.

Only now when the contracts had been passed did Sir Norman realise how greatly he had wanted this new work, how much he had longed to get his teeth into something new, to find an outlet for his activity which had been wasting itself in trivial matters.

His nerves had been strained to breaking point this last week.

For the first time a sense of responsibility began to depress him. He was almost afraid of what he had undertaken. It was so big—bigger than anything he had attempted before.

He turned away from the window and lit a cigarette. Over the mantelpiece was a small, badly executed drawing of Buller's Motor Company.

He stood looking at it for some time, then he went back to his desk and rang the bell.

It was two hours later before he left the works. He had had no luncheon, but had refused to have anything sent up to him in his office.

"My sister will be expecting me at home," he said to Miller. "I will get off as soon as we have finished and I shan't come back today. Tell the architect to get on with those plans as soon as possible. We must waste no time."

He felt already as if time was to haunt him. The very thought of 'so much to do, so little time to do it', made him say to his chauffeur, as he left the works:

"As quick as you can, Davis."

Norman Melton lived about three miles outside Melchester. His home, which had only been his for the past five years, had once belonged to an ancient county family, and flanking the drive gates were stone lions balancing an heraldic shield between their paws.

The iron gates were open and the car drove up an avenue of oak trees. The house was Georgian in design,

11

although the original foundations were several centuries older.

As the car arrived at the front door it was opened. A bell at the lodge by the gates communicated with the pantry of the house and prevented any delay on the arrival of master or guest.

"Where is Miss Melton?" Sir Norman asked the butler.

"In the morning-room, Sir Norman."

He walked across the wide hall and opened the door at the other end. His sister was sitting at her desk writing letters. She looked up when he arrived and rose to her feet.

"You are very late, Norman," she said severely.

"I couldn't get away before."

"Have you had any lunch?"

"No, I would like some."

She touched the bell and when the butler answered it, gave the necessary order.

"What time did you get up from London this morning?" she asked.

"I caught the 7.30," he said.

Alice Melton waited. She knew quite well how important his visit to London had been, that the final decision would have been taken as to whether the Melton Motor Company were to have the Government contract, but she did not ask questions.

She waited for her brother to tell her the news.

She was fond of Norman, yet she found it difficult to understand him. She was the elder by nearly ten years.

It seemed strange that they were brother and sister, for Alice had none of Norman's fire, no originality, and an entire lack of self-confidence.

Norman was a good-looking man. He was a millionaire and his personality could neither be belittled nor ignored.

'He ought to marry again,' Alice thought to herself, looking at him.

She wondered why the idea had suddenly come to her.

"We have got the contract," he said indifferently, as if he was speaking of something quite unimportant.

"I am glad," Alice answered slowly. "It will mean a lot of extra work for you, though, won't it?"

"It will, and I am glad of it," Norman answered. "I am getting stale and dull . . . and perhaps old."

Before his sister could answer, the butler announced that

12

luncheon was ready and Norman, without another word, walked from the morning-room and left her alone.

Alice made no attempt to follow him. She knew he would rather eat alone, and if he wanted further conversation with her he would come back after he had finished.

Instead she looked through the windows to where the daffodils were just beginning to come out under the trees on the lawn. They gave her very little pleasure.

When his wife had died, he had asked her to come back to him, and he had no idea how bitterly she had wept to leave the place that had been her home for so long, and which was the one dear thing to her in her life.

Norman's wife had always lived in London. On her death he had shut the London house and made up his mind to live near the works, spending all his time there, just as he had done before he was married.

He had no idea how lonely Alice found it. They had little to say to each other, having nothing in common beyond their blood relationship.

Alice made him an admirable housekeeper, and if he thought about her at all, he imagined that it was to her benefit to live with him.

He came into the room slowly, a lighted cigar between his fingers, a glass of brandy in his hand.

He settled himself by the fire before he spoke. He stretched out his long legs, sipped the brandy reflectively, then as though making a solemn pronouncement, said:

"I have decided to re-open the London house."

CHAPTER TWO

The rain was pouring down and the gutters of Shaftesbury Avenue were awash.

A few theatre-goers still stood disconsolately underneath the porticoes of the theatres, waiting for their cars, or hoping for a taxi.

The porters shut the doors inhospitably behind them, anxious to get away to their homes and their suppers.

From the stage-door which opened into one of the side-streets a girl came slowly out, calling a cheery good night to the door-keeper as she passed.

"Oh, it's raining!" she ejaculated.

"It's been doing that for the best part of two hours, Miss, and it doesn't look as if it's likely to stop."

She opened her umbrella and hurried into the rain.

She crossed the street and waited for a bus. There was a small crowd of people also waiting, all huddled under umbrellas, standing in silence, their faces turned in the same direction.

After some minutes a bus came and pulled up with a jerk. Instantly there was a scramble to get aboard it. Carlotta hurried forward, shutting her umbrella, feeling the rain beating against her face.

She stepped off the pavement; then, she was not certain how it happened—she might have slipped or been pushed by someone—she fell, slithering forward under the legs of those scrambling on to the bus.

For a moment she was too surprised to do anything. She felt helpless, afraid and drowned by the humanity about her. She struggled to regain her feet, feeling the cold wet road with her fingers.

Unexpectedly, a hand was placed under her elbow and she was hoisted up.

"I say, are you hurt?" a voice asked.

"Not at all," Carlotta started to say, but as she spoke her ankle gave under her and she cried out with pain.

"My ankle!" she said, standing on one leg, still held steady by the support of a firm hand.

The bus had already driven off and the few disappointed people who had been unable to get aboard it, and were now waiting for the next, were watching them.

"Here's a taxi, I'll help you into it."

The man who had dragged her to her feet hailed the taxi that was coming towards them. He opened the door, and half lifted, half pushed her into it.

"What's your address?" he asked.

Carlotta told him and added:

"But please don't trouble to come with me. I am quite all right."

The man did not answer her. Instead, he got into the taxi beside her, slamming the door.

"I say, you are in a mess!" he said, looking at the patch of wet which stained one side of Carlotta's red coat and at the state of her stockings and thin patent leather shoes.

"I can't think how I was so silly," she said, ruefully.

"Would you let me feel your ankle?" he asked. "I am a doctor."

She looked at her companion. He was large, broad-shouldered and clean-shaven. He had, she thought, a particularly nice voice.

There was just a faint accent in his speech, however, which she could not place; she wondered what it was, while painfully she moved her leg a little so that he could touch her ankle.

He knelt down on the floor of the taxi and felt it with expert fingers.

"I hope it is only a slight strain," he said. "Does it hurt?"

"Yes," she confessed, "there—where your fingers are now."

"A strained tendon," he said. "You must get a cold-water bandage on it at once. It might have been worse, no bones are broken—"

"I can't think how it happened," she confessed. "How I hate buses."

"So do I," he answered, "but not so much as the rain."

He took off his hat, which was dripping, and threw it on the floor in front of him and she saw that he was young—younger than she had expected.

"I am very lucky to be helped by a doctor," she said

lightly, a little embarrassed at the situation. "Usually on these occasions there's not one within twenty miles!"

"You have been unfortunate," he said; something in the way that he pronounced the words made her exclaim:

"You're Scotch, aren't you?"

"My name is Hector McCleod," he answered, and they both laughed as if it were a joke.

"Mine is Carlotta Lenshovski," she answered.

"Russian!" he exclaimed, and they laughed again.

The taxi drew up with a jerk.

"Is this right?" the taxi-driver asked doubtfully, pulling back the communicating window.

"Yes, this is right," Carlotta answered. "It always looks a bit strange at night," she added to her companion.

A huge doorway with carved stone figures round it held an imitation medieval oak door with iron studs and a barred peephole. There were no lights from the windows on either side of it or above.

Carlotta produced a Yale key, and Hector McCleod got out of the taxi and opened the door, before coming back to help her alight.

"Can you manage all right now?" he asked as she got into the shelter of the doorway.

"Won't you come in and have a drink?" she said.

He hesitated a moment.

"Are you quite certain it will be no trouble?"

"None," she assured him, "and you've been so kind." She held out her purse. "Will you please pay the taxi for me?"

"I'll do it," he said.

"But you must let me pay," Carlotta said.

He paid the man off, the rain pouring down on him as he waited for change.

"Please be sensible and let me give you the fare," Carlotta pleaded when he returned to her.

He shook his head.

"I wouldn't think of it," he replied. "It is not often I get the opportunity of rescuing a damsel in distress!"

"But I insist," she said.

"You can't insist with only one leg," he answered, with a grin. "Let me help you upstairs—if it is up we go."

He looked around him in a bewildered manner.

They were in a high, narrow hall in which he could dimly see what looked strangely like suits of armour stand-

16

ing by the walls. Carlotta hobbled on his arm to where she switched on the electric light.

"Don't look so surprised," she said as the light revealed not only suits of armour but two great show-cases filled with theatrical jewellery, wigs, feathers, and ornaments of every kind. "Surely you know this place by name, even if you have never been here before?"

He shook his head.

"I'm from the North," he apologised.

"This is Lenshovski's," Carlotta said. "Theatrical costumes. I am afraid that you will have to help me up these stairs—our rooms are at the top."

They went up the stairs slowly. When they reached the top they were in a huge room filled with dresses hanging in rows on stands. There was the faint, musty smell of worn clothes.

They passed through the room to a baize door at the end of it. Carlotta was leaning heavily on Hector's arm; her ankle was beginning to throb in a most alarming fashion.

"Are you quite sure you can manage?" he asked. "Would you like me to carry you?"

"I am all right," she answered. "Open the door, will you?"

He did as he was told and instantly Carlotta called out: "Magda! Magda! Where are you?"

A deep mellow voice answered her.

"Are you back, dearie? Supper's ready."

They passed through a small hall and opened yet another door into a room which seemed brilliantly lit in contrast, where, seated at the supper-table waiting for them, was the largest woman that Hector had ever seen in his life.

It took him some time before he could take in the details of the room, for what he saw took his breath away, it was so unexpected. It was a small room, hung from floor to ceiling with a miscellaneous collection of objects.

There were photographs, pieces of embroidery, valuable Persian carpets, Russian ikons, swords with jewelled hilts, and various trophies which could only have a sentimental value.

A log fire was blazing on the hearth. Before it in two huge arm-chairs lay an assortment of cats. There were three blue Persians, a Siamese kitten which was being singularly destructive to one of the cushions, and a ginger-coloured tabby.

The owner of this room was even more surprising than the room itself.

Magda Lenshovski must have weighed nearly twenty stone. She was a huge mountain of flesh, it was surprising that she could move at all; that she could move with agility, and quickly, was amazing.

Hector stared at her in fascination, wondering what glands were working too fast, or too slowly in her monstrous body.

She had dark hair, parted in the middle and drawn down over her ears from which hung two huge earrings of rubies set roughly in beaten gold.

She wore over her shoulders a magnificent shawl embroidered in vivid colours. She was not an ugly woman. Her eyes must once have been beautiful and they were still dark and alive beneath straight narrow eyebrows.

She rose to her feet at Carlotta's entrance.

"My dove, my angel—you are hurt!"

"I've turned my ankle," Carlotta answered. "It's only a twist."

She was holding tightly on to Hector's arm. He looked down at her and thought suddenly that she was beautiful.

She had pulled off her hat and her dark hair, curling away from her forehead, was pulled behind her uncovered ears into a mass of thick curls. Her skin was white and her dark eyes glittered as she talked.

Her body was slim and exquisite, and he realised that there was about her a strange, foreign sensuality.

'She is exotic,' he told himself, 'and the most glamourous person I've ever met.'

She took off her coat before she sat down.

She was dressed only in a simple little black dress without a touch of colour in it. Hector felt that she should have been dressed in silks, adorned with sables, bejewelled with diamonds.

There was something rich about Carlotta, and some expression in her of elegance which he sensed as he looked at her.

'She is lovely,' he thought, and almost said so aloud.

The huge woman Magda was exclaiming in her deep voice, while Carlotta chattered gaily of the accident, making a story of Hector's rescue as she was being trampled

18

to death! The incident grew in the telling, became colourful and alive.

Carlotta made Hector feel as if he had taken part in an adventure.

He dressed Carlotta's ankle, once he could make them understand that it was an immediate necessity. When he had finished, Magda invited him to join them at supper, an invitation which he was delighted to accept.

He had only to smell the delicious dishes brought to the table to know that Magda was greedy, and that she knew what was good. The Russian taste for cream, for butter, for pastry, was evident even in this short meal.

It was difficult for Hector to understand how, if she habitually enjoyed food of this sort, Carlotta was able to maintain her very fashionable, slender figure.

"A good audience tonight?" Magda asked

Hector understood then that Carlotta was an actress.

"What are you in?" he asked.

"Oh, an awful show," she replied. "It is called 'The Starry Staircase', written by one of those earnest young authors with a mission in life, whom no one wants to listen to. I'm afraid it won't run very long."

"None of the plays do these days," Magda answered. "I have no sooner dressed one show than it is off. Oh, it's good for business—as long as we get paid!"

"Trust Magda to see to that!" Carlotta interposed. "Money in advance or no costumes, is the motto of this house."

Magda laughed, a deep throaty chuckle.

"And why should I work for nothing?" she inquired.

"Oh, you are quite right," Carlotta replied. "I am only telling Mr. McCleod, or should I say doctor?"

"Have you a practice?" Magda asked.

"I am working for my London degree after taking my Scottish one," he replied. "I only came here a month ago from Edinburgh. I am at St. Anthony's."

"That's a very big hospital, isn't it?" Carlotta asked.

"One of the biggest," he answered.

"And you like doctoring?" Magda asked.

"It is the one thing I have always wanted to do ever since I was a little boy," he said. "I can hardly believe that it isn't all a dream."

"That's the way to be happy," Magda said. "To dream and to get your dream fulfilled. I once dreamt too—but many years ago."

"Magda was in the ballet," Carlotta said to Hector.

She pointed to the mantelpiece, to where, in the centre, was a pair of pink ballet shoes—they were worn and had a tired, pathetic air in their glass prison.

"I broke my leg," Magda said. "I could never dance again."

Hector didn't know what to say. There was in those few words a tragedy.

It was extraordinary, he thought, how those two women could convey just by their eyes and the expression of the face a subtle change of mood, could infuse into the conversation an atmosphere to which he could not help but respond.

He knew here was a wound deeper than any bodily hurt, and he could find no words to console, he could only listen and hope that he looked as sympathetic as he felt.

They were interrupted by the opening door and another woman came in. She was tall and thin, with curled hair of a colour which was either faded gold or dusty white.

"Hello, Leolia," Carlotta said. "Meet Dr. McCleod who has brought me home."

"Why, what has happened?" the newcomer asked.

The story of Carlotta's adventure was told once again. She sat down at the table. Hector judged that she must be nearly sixty. She too, seemed an unusual person. She was English, yet she was of no ordinary type.

When she spoke it was with the voice of an educated woman, and she had a charm which entirely belied her appearance.

"Mrs. Payne lives here with me," Magda said.

"Does she help you with the business?" Hector asked.

Leolia Payne laughed.

"There wouldn't be much of a business if I did! No, Magda runs that all herself. I only live here and look after her when Carlotta is playing in the provinces or out enjoying herself with her young men."

Carlotta laughed.

"You talk as though I was gay. I assure you, Dr. McCleod, that I generally come straight home after the theatre."

"I think you are very wise to do that," Hector answered, "if you are interested in your career."

"I am and I am not," Carlotta said, with a sigh.

"The girls these days have no ambition," Magda said. "Why, I was consumed with it, it was the only thing I

20

cared about, my dancing. We were made to practise until our toes bled, and do you think we minded . . . ?"

"Don't tell us, darling," Carlotta interrupted her. "You know that those days are past. Nowadays nobody is ambitious like that."

"Except, perhaps Norman Melton," Leolia Payne said quietly.

"Yes, perhaps Norman is," Magda answered.

A clock chimed. Hector rose to his feet to say good night; he was surprised to see how late it was. Carlotta held out her hand.

"Won't you come and see me tomorrow?" she asked. "I haven't got a matinée, and I would like my leg to be well for the evening performance."

CHAPTER THREE

Carlotta was awakened by the telephone ringing beside her bed. She stirred sleepily, then with an effort stretched out her hand and picked up the receiver.

"Hullo," she said.

"A personal call for you, Miss, from Melchester," said the voice of the boy who managed the shop exchange.

Carlotta settled herself comfortably on her pillows and waited. She knew who it was.

"Is that Miss Carlotta Lenshovski?" someone asked.

"Yes, I am speaking," she answered.

"Hold the line, please, Sir Norman Melton wishes to speak to you."

A moment later she heard Norman's voice.

"Good morning!" she said. "I thought you had forgotten all about me."

"I couldn't telephone last night," he said. "I had a conference which lasted until nearly midnight."

"So you have got the contract?" she guessed.

"I have."

There was a note of jubilation in his voice.

"Congratulations," Carlotta said, "but I never thought for a moment that you wouldn't get it. When you make up your mind, Norman, you always get what you want, don't you?"

"I might ask you to prove your belief in me," he said, then added abruptly as though he had said too much: "Will you have supper with me tonight, after the show?"

"I would love to," Carlotta answered, "that is if I go to the theatre."

"Why, what do you mean?"

She told him about her accident of the night before.

"I can't tell you how fascinating my young Scotch doctor is," she said. "He has promised to come and see me today."

"I never heard such nonsense," Sir Norman answered.

"Go to Sir Harry Andrews—he's the only man worth seeing. He's my doctor."

"I have got complete faith in my Scot," Carlotta replied. She laughed at Norman's protests.

"Don't worry," she said, "and unless you hear that I am in hospital, be waiting for me at 11.35."

"I will," he promised, "and take care of yourself, my child."

"I will do my best," she answered, and rang off.

She lay quite still for a long time watching the chinks of light through the lightly moving curtains. She was thinking of Norman.

They had met about three months ago at a cocktail party. She was introduced to Norman Melton half-way through the evening.

His name was mumbled by her hostess so that she had no idea who he was.

She found herself shaking hands with a tall, grave-looking man who seemed, somehow, out of place in the chattering, laughing throng of cocktail drinkers.

"Tell me about yourself," she said. "I expect I ought to know all about you but I must just plead ignorance."

"What do you think I am?" he asked.

Carlotta looking at him scrutinizingly, tried to guess.

"You might be a politician," she said. "You certainly aren't an actor, and I don't think you look sophisticated enough to be a diplomat. Yes, you must either be a politician or big business, or perhaps both."

Norman laughed.

"You are either a good guesser," he said, "or a flatterer."

"Then I am right?" Carlotta questioned.

"Not where politics are concerned," he answered, "but business, yes. Are you disappointed that I am not a future Prime Minister?"

Usually at these sort of functions Norman felt out of place.

He was used to intense concentration, to pouring forth his inexhaustible energy into everything he undertook, and accordingly he found it difficult to discuss trivialities at once with sincerity and that lightness relative to their unimportance.

At a dinner-party or at the luncheon-table, Norman was certain, sooner or later, to find himself enveloped in an argument.

23

In Carlotta however, he met for the first time someone in this world with whom he found it easy to converse.

He watched her face, expressively vivacious; he liked the quality of her voice, and the gestures she used to demonstrate her remarks.

She talked with her hands as well as with her lips. It was so obvious that she was not English, although she confessed to him that she could not speak any other language.

She told Norman where she was acting and he promised to come and see the play if she would have supper with him after it was over.

"I have got a rotten little part," she said, "but it is a great thing to be in the West End—the managers and agents are impressed, if not the general public."

"Why did you go on the stage?" he asked.

She shrugged her shoulders.

"Not because I had a particular call," she said, "but because I have been brought up to it. My mother—my adopted mother—is Magda Lenshovski, the theatrical costumier.

"I remember the smell of grease paint far more vividly than anything else during my childhood. I met every famous character on the boards before I was five, for I used to go to rehearsals when Magda had to arrange the dresses.

"In fact, my first lessons were memorising the parts I heard repeated over and over again, as I sat in the empty stalls waiting for Magda to come from the dressing-rooms.

"I couldn't say 'no', when Christian Holden offered me a part in his company. I was just seventeen and I thought him the most attractive man I had ever seen in my life. Of course I accepted—who wouldn't have?"

"Is there anything else you would rather have done?" Norman asked.

"Oh, nothing particular," Carlotta answered. "I think I am just lazy. I don't really want to do anything in life except enjoy myself. Now you can't understand that, can you?"

She knew by this time who he was and she remembered reading about him in the newspapers, of his sensational rise until he became director and owner of the factory in which he had gone to work as a boy.

"I have been driven by my ambition all my life," Norman confessed. "That sounds rather as though I was giving a newspaper interview, but, strangely enough, it's true."

"Are you content now?" Carlotta asked.

He laughed abruptly.

"I haven't even started," he answered.

They dined together the following night and Carlotta decided that she liked him.

His keen intelligence appealed to her, and she was amused by his abrupt, at times almost rude, manner, which was obviously assumed to conceal his shyness.

She could quite understand why some people disliked and misunderstood him, but she herself had lived too long amongst all sorts of people to judge by surface superficialities.

"It's funny," she said later to Magda, "but in some ways I feel as though he's younger than I am. He is so unsophisticated about everything except his motors."

She was sitting on Magda's bed as she spoke, a vast mahogany four-poster. She wore a white tulle dress with silver sequin shoulder straps, and she looked very young and amazingly lovely. Magda understood what she meant.

"You're Russian!" she replied. "We are as old as God."

"Only half," Carlotta answered, "you forget my father."

"I never knew him," Magda said with a twinkle.

"I wonder what he was like?" Carlotta said.

Getting off the bed she walked towards the huge looking-glass.

"I expect he was tall and fair and stupid," Magda replied, "like most Englishmen."

"Was the one you loved like that?" Carlotta asked.

Magda did not reply for a moment. She was propped up on her pillows, her huge body under the bedclothes lay like a mountain before her. She peered at Carlotta with dark, suspicious eyes.

"What do you mean?" she asked.

"Don't pretend," Carlotta answered. "Leolia told me! Oh, years ago! You mustn't be angry because I wormed it out of her."

"I never think about him," Magda answered.

"That's a lie!" Carlotta said. "But never mind, let's go on talking about me, if you prefer it. Am I like my mother?"

"You are," Magda replied.

"Then she must have been very pretty," Carlotta said.

"She wasn't when I saw her," Magda answered. "She had been without food for two days. She was white and drawn and her eyes were dark hollows in her head."

"And yet she was lovely," Carlotta answered. "I know she was lovely—tell me so."

"She must have been a very beautiful woman," Magda said shortly.

"And she was a Romanoff," Carlotta said in a voice of triumph. "A Romanoff! Do you think I am worthy of her?"

"You'll do," said Magda in a gruff voice which hid the deep affection for the child she had brought up. "Get to bed, you will be tired in the morning if you don't. When's this fine young man of yours coming to take you out again?"

"Tomorrow night, perhaps," Carlotta answered. "I think he likes me."

"More fool he if he doesn't," Magda replied. "Bring him to see me one day and I will tell you what I think of him."

"As long as you don't tell him what you think," Carlotta said, "I will bring him, but not unless you promise."

She was half laughing, half serious, for she had suffered in the past from Magda's frankness.

The old woman had no compunction about expressing her mind, regardless of whether it was pleasant to hear or not.

Magda was a character; the whole theatrical world knew that; some loved her, some hated her, but all in the profession were forced to accept her.

The designers adored her, for she was so artistic that she never allowed anything ugly or inappropriate to leave her work-rooms.

She did not mind when people laughed at her, and when an angry juvenile lead nicknamed her 'The Ugly Duchess', she bore him no ill-feeling.

The name had stuck and to the theatrical world Magda was 'The Ugly Duchess'. She grew used to hearing people refer to her in this way and even, on occasion, used the nickname herself.

Perhaps it was Magda's huge body before her that made Carlotta crave beauty. She wanted to be lovely from the time when she was a tiny child.

She hated anything which was not attractive, crying out

in fear from a golliwog that had been given to her, and hating toys which were not dainty in appearance.

As she grew older she refused to wear clothes that did not appeal to her artistic sense or satisfy her taste.

"When I grow up," she told Magda when she was five, "I am going to be as beautiful as an angel."

Magda had laughed at the child's remark, but to Carlotta it was the registration of a vow of which she was to be conscious all through the years.

So the child grew up.

She blossomed into a lovely person, so lovely that at times Magda stared at her in amazement.

Carlotta had been nervous when, after accepting nearly a dozen invitations from Norman Melton, she had invited him home to meet Magda.

"She's a strange person," she warned him. "If she doesn't like you she may say so outright! She will certainly show her feelings very obviously!"

She was faintly amused to see that Norman was nervous. It seemed funny that this clever man, rich and successful, should be afraid of a gross old woman with an alarming tongue.

Socially, Magda was poles apart from the motor millionaire, yet their link was Carlotta, and she saw herself as a bridge between them.

It was a close, foggy evening and Magda's sitting-room was stuffy.

The old woman was sitting with a red shawl draped over her shoulders, with heavy rings in her ears which glittered every time she moved her head, her wrists weighed down with Oriental bangles of gold and silver.

She looked fantastic. There was a cat sitting in her vast lap and two others ranged at her feet.

She did not attempt to get up but held out her hand to Norman as imperiously as an Empress might have done, and gave him one of her quick, speculative glances.

Carlotta knew that she was summing him up, making up her mind instinctively.

Just for a moment, Carlotta felt anxious; she liked Norman, it was not often she wanted Magda's approval, but was afraid of her antagonism.

"Supper is ready," Magda said.

There was a note of approval in her voice. Carlotta recognised it.

She felt immensely relieved.

CHAPTER FOUR

Hector McCleod walked jauntily out of the hospital and stopped at the nearest telephone box.

He looked up a number under 'L', dialled rapidly, pressed button 'A', and asked for Miss Carlotta Lenshovski.

It was some time before he heard her voice.

"Who is it?" she inquired.

"Hector McCleod," he said. "How are you today—is the ankle better?"

"Oh, it's you," she said. "The boy got in such a muddle over your name, I couldn't think who it was."

"He'll get to know it in time," Hector promised her. "And the ankle?"

"It's much better," she said. "I am keeping it up all this afternoon and I think I shall only limp a tiny bit tonight."

"Must you use it at all?" he asked.

"I can't be carried on to do my part," she laughed.

"I mean, can't you take the evening off?"

She laughed again at his ignorance.

"With only five appearances and a few lines to say," she said, "they don't run to an understudy for my part. If I don't turn up I shall more than likely get the sack."

"Well, may I come round and see you?" he asked.

"Not if you are going to say that it is your considered professional opinion that I should stay in bed."

"I won't, I promise you," he said. "I will come entirely as a friend, if I may."

"Come to tea at 4.30," Carlotta invited.

"I'll be there on the stroke," he said eagerly.

He had an hour and a half to wait. He looked at his watch and checked it with an adjacent church. Then he sauntered down the dingy, over-crowded streets surrounding the hospital, towards the West End.

To all appearances Hector was a sturdy, unemotional Scot. Those who worked with him thought him of imperturbable humour, pleasant but dull.

28

They had no idea that beneath an easy, confident manner, he suffered with all the sensitiveness of a man deeply emotional by nature and working now abnormally hard without proper nourishment.

It was not easy to live on the very small sum a week that Hector allowed himself. He had a hearty appetite which he had always been used to appeasing at a plentiful table.

In London he was invariably hungry. There was never a moment when he could not have eaten more and eaten it greedily. But hungry and lonely, he was still happy.

So grateful was he to the circumstances which had got him to where he was that he would not allow himself to complain.

Nevertheless, it had been a welcome break to meet Carlotta the night before.

The men with whom he was working at the hospital were most of them London men who had many friends and many interests outside their work.

They were on the whole delightful fellows, but Hector did not room with any of them, and at the end of a month they remained acquaintances with whom he had only medical practise in common.

Carlotta was the first person outside the hospital with whom he had had a real conversation for nearly six weeks. He had enjoyed his supper and he wanted to see her again.

All the morning while he had been at work in the laboratory he had been debating with himself whether he dared take her at her word to come again.

At the afternoon lecture he had found it difficult to concentrate on what the lecturer was saying. More than once he missed a sentence or two as he asked himself:

'Did she really mean it? Shall I telephone or just turn up?'

The fear of being sent away made him decide to telephone, and as he left the box he was elated out of all proportion to think that once again he would meet these new friends.

'She's lovely,' he told himself, and in spite of himself he said the same thing aloud when he saw Carlotta.

He had meant to tell her that she looked well, but instead he found himself stammering: "You look lovely," as she received him in Magda's congested sitting-room, holding out her hand in welcome from the sofa arranged in the window.

She was wearing a dress of some soft blood-red material trimmed with touches of sable at the wrist and neck. Her only jewellery was a large cross of gold and rubies hung from a narrow black ribbon.

"I am resting, you see," she said. "Don't tell me I don't obey doctor's orders."

She was amused at his stammered greeting, at the same time his boyish embarrassment after the words had escaped him, made her feel shy too.

With Norman Melton, Carlotta had felt old and sophisticated. With Hector, only a few years her senior, she felt young and inexperienced. She dropped her eyes before his.

There was a strained silence before he said:

"May I look at your ankle?"

He touched it and found there was only a slight swelling.

"It only aches a little," Carlotta said. "It will be well by tomorrow."

"You will have to take it easy for a day or two," Hector answered. "I did the same thing one summer and it was nearly a week before I was perfectly well."

"I will be very careful," she said meekly.

Tea was brought up by a servant and as it was put on the table, Hector poured out, bringing a cup to Carlotta's side and handing her sandwiches and cakes.

She only played with her food, watching him as he wolfed down a whole plate of sandwiches and had two or three helpings of cake before he noticed that he was eating alone.

"I say, am I being greedy?" he asked.

"What did you have for lunch?" she said.

"Oh, I don't have any," he answered, "I don't get time. I get breakfast and supper—I find it better to work on two meals a day."

Carlotta frowned at him.

"And you call yourself a doctor," she said. "You must be mad. How can anybody work if they haven't had enough to eat?"

Hector laughed.

"Oh, I don't manage so badly," he said. "Besides, all the experts will tell you that we eat too much these days. Soon we shall be able to exist on a lettuce leaf and an occasional orange."

"It's ridiculous!" Carlotta said. "I shall tell Magda."

"What will you tell her?" came from a deep voice in the doorway.

"Oh, it's Dr. McCleod," Magda said, coming slowly into the room.

"He's starving himself to death," Carlotta announced.

Magda looked at him severely.

"If it's true, you are a very silly young man," she said.

"Only a poor one," Hector expostulated, but flushing a little, he hated to talk of money. "Things are very expensive in London, you know, and I'm Scottish enough to like value for my money."

"There's always a meal here at any reasonable hour," Magda said gruffly, helping herself liberally to toast and butter.

"That's very kind of you," Hector answered.

"Now, don't forget," Carlotta said. "When Magda invites anybody to a meal she means them to come and enjoy it. She never gives out polite invitations—do you, darling?"

Magda looked at Hector and liked him. She understood an ambition which would not be thwarted, even by privation.

She rose laboriously to her feet.

"I shall expect you to supper tomorrow night," she said to Hector. "You can have it with me if Carlotta is out."

"I shall be honoured," he said, holding the door open for her.

"You will be disappointed, you mean," she answered sharply disappearing through the baize door into the shop.

CHAPTER FIVE

Norman walked slowly up the stairs of Number 225 Belgrave Square.

He resented the memories of the past which his former home awoke in him. Everything was vividly reminiscent of his wife.

Evelyn had decorated it to her taste and chosen the furniture piece by piece, but it seemed to Norman that he was as alien to the house he owned as he had once been to the woman he had married.

He had been too busy after Evelyn's death to think often of the years they had spent together. He owned, when he was honest with himself, that her death had caused him no regrets; indeed, it gave him a sense of relief.

He had been afraid of his wife. Never would he admit it, yet deep in his heart he knew it to be the truth.

She frightened him, and she had made little effort to destroy the barriers which had quickly arisen between them, even on their brief honeymoon.

Lady Evelyn Cleeve had been the widowed daughter of the Earl of Brora, an old man who ruled the family castle and its few remaining acres with the iron hand of the autocrat.

He had insisted on the marriage, when he had become aware that Norman was courting his daughter.

Evelyn had married Colin Cleeve in the middle of the War and had known one blissful year of happiness, before he had been shot down by an enemy aeroplane.

Colin had been a strange person, a mixture of poet and adventurer. He had captivated Evelyn and she had loved him without restraint. When he had been killed she felt as though all that mattered in life had been taken from her.

She was bitter, resentful, and broken. She would not rouse herself even to care for the child that he had left her.

The girl had been born at the beginning of 1918, seven months after Colin was killed.

Evelyn christened her Skye, partly in a kind of pathetic tribute to the element in which her husband had met his death, partly because the happiest days of her childhood had been spent in the misty isles where her father had owned a small lodge.

In her widowhood Evelyn Cleeve retired to Glenholme Castle to keep house for her father. She let life drift languidly past, taking no interest in what was occurring outside the strath in which the Castle was situated.

She had been gay and a somewhat impulsive girl; in widowhood she became a dull, reserved woman.

But she was good-looking, almost beautiful in a cold, distinguished manner.

To Norman Melton meeting her for the first time, she seemed the embodiment of everything aristocratic, everything, indeed, which he himself was not.

He had been asked up to Scotland by a business acquaintance, who had taken the shooting on an adjacent moor to the Glenholme Estate. They had gone over to the Castle for tea one Sunday afternoon.

Sitting in the high room watching Evelyn pour out the tea, her slim hands moving deftly among the valuable china and precious family silver, Norman felt as though he had been transported into one of the historical romances he had read as a boy.

Evelyn was wearing a plain dress of some dark-blue material. She wore no jewellery, and her hair was drawn back from her white forehead into an unfashionable but becoming knot, at the nape of her neck.

Looking at her, trying to think of something that he could say to interest her, the extraordinary thought came to his mind that here was the woman he should marry.

He felt with an amazing clarity of mind that here was the one asset he lacked and needed.

"I have brains, push and money," he told himself. "She has breeding and beauty."

He hardly dared to express, even to himself, the thought that their children might be magnificent as a result of such a balanced combination. He could not think of her in the terms of ordinary human passion.

At the same time, his mind was made up. He was sure about Evelyn, as swiftly and decisively as he was sure when a business deal was put before him.

'I want her,' he told himself, then changed the sentence to: 'I will have her.'

He set himself to be charming, not only to Evelyn but to her father. He judged the old man shrewdly, flattered him by an attentive deference, and guessed the right methods by which to arouse his interest.

He succeeded in getting himself asked to stay at Glenholme for a week's shooting.

Evelyn had been quite unprepared for the siege he laid to her affections. She had grown used to thinking of herself as though, almost, she were disembodied.

Every night she would pray for nearly an hour before she went to bed, offering a supplication to God for the husband she had lost.

She believed that in this way she could still communicate with that beloved person. She was comforted by the habit. It was the only expression of feeling left to her, the only desire which had not been disciplined into a colourless routine.

At her prayers she felt near to Colin; felt that death was not the end; that he was waiting for her somewhere beyond the grave . . .

She had his poems. Four slim books, two written while he was at Oxford and two later when he was in no hurry to find himself work.

She knew them by heart, the dramatic outpourings of a man who was groping for something which he sensed, yet could not capture into understanding.

When Evelyn first began to realise that Norman was attracted by her, she shrank in revulsion from him, feeling that he violated her, even by the implication that she was an attractive woman.

It was as if he offered an insult to Colin.

"I have a husband," Evelyn told herself passionately.

She could never think of herself as a widow.

But Norman knew when he had made a false step. After his first tentative overtures, he made no further mention of affection, much less of love. He seemed to offer Evelyn an impersonal friendship.

From being horrified at his presumption in loving her, Evelyn was piqued at the way he responded to her first rebuff.

She told herself she had misunderstood him, and was consumed by curiosity as to whether or not she had been mistaken.

In the meantime her father had made inquiries about Norman. Lord Brora was greatly impressed by what he heard, and actually the tales of Norman's brilliance and of his growing fortune were not unduly exaggerated.

They certainly made an excellent report for a prospective father-in-law, who was finding that the burdens of increasing taxation were almost overwhelming.

"I like the man," Lord Brora said to his daughter. "He's got guts and he's got brains. You could do a lot worse."

"I shall never marry again," Evelyn told him quietly.

"When I am dead," her father said, "you will have precious little to live on, for this place and every penny I possess will go to Arthur's son. I can't leave you anything, you know that."

"I have got Colin's money," Evelyn answered.

"A paltry five hundred a year!" her father snorted. "That won't help you much, especially with a child on your hands."

Evelyn frowned, faintly disturbed. She was well aware that if she considered Norman in relation to Skye, the problem of her remarriage took on a different complexion altogether.

The child was getting to the age when she required either a good governess or to be sent to a first-class school. There was at present neither the money nor the facilities for either.

With Skye's education and her father's anxiety for the future balanced in Norman's favour, Evelyn hesitated before she definitely sent him away, and in her hesitation was lost.

She could not withstand her father's urging and she liked Norman. He was physically attractive to her, even while she denied it, and told herself that no man should ever take Colin's place.

Finally she capitulated and they were married. Having committed herself she was docile and willing until the actual day of the ceremony.

Then something bitter and revengeful in her heart, something which lusted to hurt her lover as she had been hurt at Colin's death, rose to make between herself and Norman an animosity which neither could overcome.

Evelyn struggled to overcome her own nature, to be at least grateful to her husband for his generosity, but she found it impossible not to hate him for what he gave her.

She loathed the jewellery that he heaped upon her because it had not come from Colin. She disliked the unlimited money she could spend on houses, on furniture and on clothes.

She wanted, with a passion that surprised herself, to share these things only with the past, with Colin, the husband she had loved, not with the man who offered them to her now.

She was frightened at the violence of her own feelings; so frightened that she controlled herself with a severity which never for a moment allowed her reserve to lighten.

Only with Skye did Norman find happiness during his married life. He had loved his little stepdaughter from the first moment he saw her.

She was not in the least like her mother in looks, being very short, round-limbed, and plump. She had laughing grey eyes and bright-red hair, which she had inherited from her father.

Evelyn had made in the first months of their marriage, some attempt to get her daughter to call Norman 'Beaupère, or one of the other conventional names usually given to stepfathers, but Skye had insisted on calling him Norman.

It had tickled him and made him feel young. He invariably did feel young in Skye's company, almost in contrast to the time spent with Evelyn, when he was made to feel immeasurably old. His wife had a deadening effect on him, his stepdaughter stimulated him.

Until he knew Skye, he had not realised that he was fond of children.

When Evelyn died he had asked Skye to continue to live with him, but Lord Brora had insisted on her going back to the Castle for her holidays, and Norman had not the heart to take her away from school.

She was happy there and he continued to pay the considerable fees every term, even though by doing so he was deprived of her company.

He went down to see her as often as he could during term-time, and he looked forward to his visits as much, if not more, than she did.

When Skye was eighteen, she told Norman that when she was in London she wished to share a flat with a friend rather than stay with him. He was bitterly disappointed, for he had planned to reopen his house in Belgrave Square for her.

But he was wise enough to understand that she sought

independence, and he gave in to her wishes without argument.

Skye had grown up with the desire for self-expression which must in some ways have been a reaction from her mother's repression.

She was always sweet, frank, and affectionate with her stepfather, but their interests lay in different directions, and he knew that they could never mean to each other all he had hoped while she was still a child under his protection.

Walking into the big drawing-room on the first floor in Belgrave Square, Norman remembered the last time he had been there had been for Skye's coming-out dance.

It was the first time he had opened the house since his wife's death, but he had so many guests there that night that he found it difficult to think seriously, or to reminisce.

While he stood thinking on the landing, he heard a gay voice hail him from downstairs.

"Norman! Norman! Where are you?"

He leant over the bannisters, looked down into the deep well of the staircase, and saw his stepdaughter staring up at him.

"Skye!" he exclaimed in surprise. "What are you doing here?"

"I was passing, darling," she explained. "I saw your car outside, and guessed you were making a tour of inspection."

"Come up!" he said abruptly.

She obeyed him, running up the stairs two at a time. She held out her arms in greeting.

"I am pleased to see you," she said, kissing him affectionately on both cheeks.

She was so small that he had to stoop down to her. He held her at arm's length, looking at her with quizzical eyes.

"You're looking well," he said grudgingly. "Chelsea suits you."

"I might almost say the same of Melchester," she replied. "But what's the idea of being here?"

"I was just looking round," he said guiltily.

Skye looked at him scrutinizingly.

"Darling," she said, "you are lying! You are thinking of getting married again!"

CHAPTER SIX

Skye had often wondered in what way she resembled her mother.

'There must,' she thought, 'be some link between mother and child, which, sooner or later, will express itself.'

But up to date she could find nothing in herself which she recognised as part of Evelyn Cleeve's character or personality.

Skye was very small and there is something about a tiny woman which makes every man with whom she comes in contact eager to protect her. Her loveliness she took as a matter of course and generally forgot to make the most of herself.

In Scotland she was dazzling; in London she was often surpassed by others who took trouble with their clothes and with their faces.

Skye liked old clothes, comfortable shoes, and the society of intelligent people.

She loved more than anything the free life in Scotland; the moors, the hills, the cascading burns, and the river winding past Glenholme.

She could not, however, for long stand the atmosphere of age and sheltered peace, which was as much a part of her grandfather's household as he was himself.

She was driven by a conviction within herself—that she must stand alone and be self-sufficient.

She knew, too, that she could not find such independence in Norman's household; he offered her a too luxurious and too comfortable an existence.

While she had been growing up she had tried to talk to her mother, to find the answers or some explanation to the questions which puzzled her. But Evelyn had failed her daughter.

Norman, with his direct approach to life, fascinated Skye. He taught her far more useful lessons than any she learnt at school.

It was Norman who discovered that Skye had an eye for colour, and encouraged her to persevere at her painting.

When Skye finally decided that she must live her own life, she went to Chelsea, determined to spend at least two years studying art.

The only condition both Norman and her grandfather made in consenting to her plans was she should share a flat with some girl considerably older than herself and someone of whom they approved.

It was fortunate, therefore, that a distant cousin of Evelyn's, who was making quite a considerable income out of decorative work, was prepared to take Skye in as a lodger, for, as she expressed it, a trial run.

The experiment was a complete success. Mary Glenholme was nearly forty, she was plain, sensible, humourous when the mood took her, and responsible enough to satisfy both Lord Brora and Norman.

The latter, taking her out to luncheon alone, confided his anxieties for Skye's future, and was reassured by Mary's sound common sense.

"Give her her head now, when she wants it," she said, "and you will have no trouble in the future! But if you don't she will break out sooner or later and there will be the devil to pay. She's not a limp, languid body like Evelyn was.

"You must forgive me saying so, but after Colin's death she was a dead woman, and you know it! Skye's got both character and personality. I will watch over her for you— but not so that she notices it."

"I hope you will!" Norman answered apprehensively.

"You are like a fussy old hen with one chick!" Mary said, "and Skye's grandfather's as bad! You should have heard the questions he asked me about my life. You would have thought that Chelsea was Sodom and Gomorrah rolled into one."

"Is there much licence in Chelsea?" Norman asked, "or is that just an atmosphere created by newspapers and novelists?"

Mary gave a deep guffaw of choking amusement.

"You must forgive my natural anxiety," Norman said.

"You're all the same," she said. "You think that because an artist has a paint brush in one hand he must hold a glass of absinthe in the other. My dear man, Chelsea nowadays is as respectable as South Kensington, and a damn' sight more so than Mayfair.

39

"You can take it from me the small amount of vice and free love that there is in Chelsea is always amongst those who pretend to be artists rather than those that are."

Norman would have been surprised if he had realised how ambitious Skye was for him.

He had no idea that his stepdaughter was desperately anxious for him to succeed in all his undertakings, and that she had already made up her mind that he must eventually be one of the most influential business men in the British Isles.

She knew, of course, that had she been a boy there would have been a place for her in Norman's works, and that on his retirement she might have been able to take over the business if he had not produced a son.

As it was, there was no active part that she could play in his affairs. She could only listen.

Norman would often discuss things with her, and if she could not help him, in her ignorance, because he could talk of his difficulties, they would often be clarified for him.

She appreciated his confidence, but those were the times when she bitterly regretted her sex.

"Norman ought to have a son," she told Mary. "It would give him something to work for—not that he really needs much encouragement, but I suppose that every man wants to hand over an inheritance to his own flesh and blood."

"He will have to marry again, then," Mary answered. "I hope he chooses the right person this . . ."

She checked herself, but Skye knew only too well what she was going to say.

". . . this time," she finished for her. "You needn't pretend, Mary, I know that Mummy was absolutely the wrong person for Norman. You couldn't imagine two people with less in common.

"Mummy made Norman feel awkward; I used to watch him fidgeting because she was present, and feel so terribly sorry for him. Yes, I hope he marries someone really sweet and kind."

Passing Belgrave Square on her way home from a luncheon party, she had seen Norman's car outside Number 225.

Skye did not know quite why the sight of her stepfather at the top of the stairs told her that he was contemplating anything so serious as remarriage, yet, instinctively, she felt it was so.

It seemed to her imagination that he was not alone, but with him, as he smiled a greeting, was the vivid oval face she had seen beside him in the car.

"Tell me the truth!" she commanded him.

She knew by his hesitation and by the awkward words of denial that finally came to his lips that she had, though he would not admit it, been entirely correct in her presumption.

"You're making romantic mountains out of commonplace molehills," Norman said. "I am here because I shall have to be in London a good deal in the future and I have decided to reopen the house."

"How lovely," Skye said. "I hate to think of it all shuttered and barred. The poor old thing—it looks lonely, doesn't it? But you must do it up, darling."

"Just what I thought of doing," Norman said. "You will have to help me."

"Perhaps my taste won't suit your bride-to-be," Skye teased.

"I have already told you," Norman said decisively, "that I have no intention of marrying again."

"I saw you the other night," Skye said.

"When? Where?" Norman said abruptly.

"She was very lovely. What is her name?"

"Who?" Norman asked.

Then catching Skye's eyes, he realised that she was determined in her curiosity, and he laughed.

"All right," he said. "I will tell you if you want to know. Her name is Carlotta. She's on the stage and she's the adopted daughter of Magda Lenshovski."

"What, that enormous woman who dressed all the plays?" Skye asked. "I know her, of course. I always hire my dress from her for the Chelsea Arts Ball."

"That's the one," Norman said. "And Carlotta is her adopted daughter."

"Is she nice?" Skye asked. "And is she clever? Norman, darling, you mustn't marry a fool, however pretty she is."

"I'm not going to marry her," Norman answered. "I haven't even asked her."

"But you are thinking of it, aren't you? Oh, Norman, my sweet, do be very careful to choose someone who will help you. Will she like Melchester? You have got to think of that."

"I will think of it," Norman said. "Don't you worry."

"But of course I worry," Skye replied. "You don't

imagine for a moment that you can look after yourself, do you?"

"I had always imagined," Norman answered, "that I was doing it rather successfully."

They both laughed.

"Anything new to tell me?" Skye asked.

"I have got the Government contract," Norman answered.

Skye threw her arms round his neck and kissed him.

"Oh, darling, how marvellous!" she said. "I hardly dared to ask you in case it was still undecided. After all these months it is really signed and sealed?"

"It's signed," he said, "and we start work right away. It's a stupendous job—you realise that?"

"But of course!" Skye replied. "But not too stupendous for you. Nothing could be—could it? You wouldn't like to take me into the business with you, I suppose, and let me help you with it?"

Norman put a hand under her chin and tilted her face up to his.

"We shouldn't get any of the work done," he said, "with you in the factory, and that's a compliment."

Skye made a grimace.

"Not the sort I want," she said. "It is absolutely damnable that if you are a woman the only thing men consider important about you is how you look! And if one does succeed in doing anything intelligent, they ignore it, or say: 'Why bother when you are pretty?' Sometimes I wish I had warts and a squint."

"Never mind," Norman answered. "You will appreciate yourself one day when you find someone you want to look really lovely for. How are all the young men, by the way?"

"Awful!" Skye answered. "I leave Mary to cope with them, they whine and get maudlin. I can't think why I can't find a young man like you, darling, full of ambition and brains."

"There must be plenty of them about," her stepfather answered.

By this time they had wandered downstairs to the smoking-room. Skye curled her legs under her in a big armchair, Norman faced her across the hearth.

"Now don't let's talk about me," she said. "Tell me everything you are doing, about the new factories, the machines, and the contract. Tell me everything—right from the beginning, where we left off."

And Norman, spurred on by her enthusiasm, did as he was told.

Norman had paid no heed to Skye's warning about the risks of remarriage.

In spite of his common sense and his reasoning which told him that he was being ridiculous, he knew that he wanted Carlotta more than he had ever wanted anything in his life before.

He had fallen in love with her the first time that they met, and each time he saw her he found himself captured and ensnared the more irrevocably by her charm and loveliness.

He tried at first to fight the feelings which surged through him when he met her, to quell by will power the tumult of emotion which the mere touch of her hand aroused in him.

"This is madness! I will ask her to supper for the last time," he said to himself.

But on each occasion he knew that he must see her again.

He was well aware that had he been a younger man, had he belonged to Carlotta's generation, he would before now have proposed marriage. That he had refrained from speaking the words which hovered on his lips was not solely due to caution.

He had forced himself to keep silent, to leave those words unspoken, not because he was afraid of her answer, but because he believed in attacking this problem as he attacked every other in his life, by business-like methods.

He wanted to arouse first in Carlotta a genuine interest towards himself before he offered her a half-share in his life. He would leave her, the words of love trembling on his lips because he believed that the right moment was not yet.

When Skye had gone from the house in Belgrave Square Norman half regretted that he had not been frank, had not enlisted her sympathy and her understanding in what seemed to him the most difficult task he had ever undertaken.

She might, he thought now, with feminine intuition have told him what was the way to approach Carlotta, perhaps to sweep her off her feet, as he had been swept off his. But his natural shyness had prevented him from being honest.

As Skye said good-bye and kissed him, she said:

"Good hunting, darling! I hope she says yes."

43

"You are ridiculous," Norman answered her abruptly.

"I am?" she questioned. "I shall wait and see."

And he knew that his procrastination had not convinced her.

'Skye has almost a clairvoyant presentiment at times,' he thought.

He had often found that true, and also that she was amazingly right in any line of action she propounded. Now he had the impulse to run after her, to ask her to come back and talk things over.

His natural reticence asserted itself. He went back into the house. Sitting in the smoking-room he smoked three cigarettes in succession, his forehead knit in a frown, his expression one of intense concentration.

After nearly an hour had passed, he went to the telephone. Carlotta answered him herself.

"I want to see you," he said. "What are you doing now?"

"Oh, I am frightfully busy," she answered, "and you'll laugh when I tell you what I am doing."

"Well, what are you?" he asked.

"I am sticking my press cuttings into a book," she replied. "I think it will be nice for my grandchildren to see how brilliant Grannie was in the early thirties."

"Must you worry about the grandchildren at the moment?" Norman asked. "I want you to come round here."

"Where's here?"

"I am at my house in Belgrave Square," he said. "I told you I was thinking of reopening it, and I want your advice about the decorations."

There was a little pause.

"I'd love to help you," Carlotta said. "But not now. I am covered with paste and I can't be bothered to change. Come and have tea with me instead."

Norman wanted to argue, instead he said:

"I will come right away."

He had wanted Carlotta to see the house. He was disappointed; at the same time, relieved.

He was afraid of seeing her in Evelyn's place, afraid that in Belgrave Square she would appear a different person from the one he loved in her own strange Bohemian background.

Driving towards the Strand he found himself planning, as he had so often done before, his future. He saw Carlotta at 'The Paddocks', in Belgrave Square; he tried to visualise

44

their life together; to imagine himself happily married—perhaps the father of a family.

Always the picture was unsatisfactory, incomplete. He saw the factory grasping out towards him, demanding his time, his brain, his attention.

He saw Carlotta, in spite of anything he could offer her, finding 'The Paddocks' inadequate, Belgrave Square as gloomy as he had once found it.

'Such a marriage is impossible,' he told himself abruptly as he had done a thousand times before.

As he stood outside Magda's fantastic, over-ornamented front door, Norman sighed. He wondered if Carlotta really wanted to see him. Why should she?

He had lost, he knew, what really mattered in life; the enthusiasm of youth for an ideal.

Carlotta, as she had told Norman, was working at her press-cutting book.

She had, by putting the newspaper cuttings when they arrived into a drawer, got many months behind with the sequence of dates.

She had meant to stick them in on the first rainy day, but always, when that day came, she found something else more important or attractive to do.

This afternoon she had taken them all out, and was horrified to find how much there was to be done.

She started clipping the cuttings tidily with a pair of scissors, pasting on an old *Tatler*, then arranging them neatly in the large green scrap-book marked with her name.

Carlotta had managed in her short stage career to have a great deal more publicity than her acting warranted, but she was peculiarly photogenic and the editors of magazines were often delighted to include a photograph of her on their pages solely for its artistic merits.

Carlotta, turning back the pages of her scrap-book, looked at herself critically. She could not help but be pleased by some of the reproductions of herself.

She did indeed look amazingly beautiful in many of them, and what mattered to Carlotta even more than beauty was that, however extraordinary the pose, she had nevertheless a quality in herself which prevented her from being cheap.

Carlotta told herself proudly it was the unmistakable evidence of good breeding. Carlotta, brought up as she had been by Magda in the easy, hail-fellow-well-met manner of the theatrical world, was a snob.

Of course, not even to her dearest and closest friends would she have ever admitted it, but what mattered to her more than anything else, was that her mother had been a Romanoff.

The story of her actual birth was romantic enough to fire her imagination. Carlotta's mother had been helped in her escape in the Bolshevik revolution by a young Englishman.

For some days they had been unable to cross the frontier, and during that time had fallen deeply in love with each other.

Finally, they had made their escape and had travelled on a cattle steamer across the Black Sea to Constantinople.

Here, they had for a moment been unable to proceed farther, and they had lived together in Constantinople as man and wife, unnoticed among the terrified, starving throng of refugees.

After a great deal of delay, they reached Paris, and having found a temporary home for the woman he had rescued, Carlotta's father crossed to England.

He had been wounded in the early stages of the war and had returned to the Diplomatic profession which he had renounced to serve in the Army.

Having promised Carlotta's mother he would send for her at the first possible opportunity, he reported to the Foreign Office and was faced with the news that he was ordered immediately to New York on an important mission.

He had no time to do more than write a brief line of farewell before he caught his boat.

Broken-hearted by what she believed was his desertion, Carlotta's mother did not answer the letter and shortly afterwards left Paris for England.

By this time she was aware that she was going to have a child and she felt that in a France at war and so dangerously near to defeat it was no place to have it.

She missed, by this movement, the letters which she should have received from America, for during the interval of weeks which it took for a ship to cross the Atlantic and for the mails to travel back to Europe.

She had lost all heart and was quite certain that she would never see the man she loved again. She had no idea what she was to do when her small amount of money came to an end.

However, she set out for England, feeling that she must find friends, perhaps relations, in that country where she had stayed when she was a girl and of which she had such pleasant memories.

Only when she reached London did she feel that she might not be welcomed with open arms, bearing the child of an Englishman who had apparently deserted her.

For the first time she was afraid for herself socially. She had not thought of conventions before.

Her escape from the people who had killed her father and mother before her eyes, the days and weeks of fear and starvation, of battling for life itself, had made her think only of her desire for self-preservation. But now she was afraid.

Her family were exceedingly proud. The relations with whom she had stayed in the past years held a high position. Quite suddenly she felt she could not meet them again, could not face them in her present condition.

She wandered hopelessly down the Strand, wondering what she should do. She turned up a side street, and the sight of a Russian name inscribed above a queer-looking shop attracted her attention—'Lenshovski'. She went in at the door and found Magda.

"I want work," she told her.

When Magda shook her head, for she had nothing for her, the Russian girl sat down on a chair and burst into tears.

Things happened rapidly after that. She found herself in Magda's private room with the first cup of good Russian tea she had enjoyed since she left St. Petersburg.

They were talking together as two women in exile, as two friends might who had not met for a long time.

Each called up in the other a wave of overwhelming homesickness and at the end of an hour Magda had agreed to take the stranger not only into her shop, but into her home.

Carlotta was born on one cold October morning, when the wind was whistling round the windows and down the chimney, and the sky was grey and overcast.

The doctor called hurriedly in consultation told Magda the truth.

"It is quite impossible to save the mother," he said.

Magda muttered miserably under her breath.

"She is quite conscious," he said, "but it is a question of hours only. Nothing we can do can save her."

Magda went in to the woman who had become a very dear friend throughout the months they had been together.

She was lying back exhausted in the great four-poster bed. Her face, drained of all blood, was whiter than the pillow on which she lay. As Magda approached she beckoned the nurse and asked her for the baby.

When they brought it to her, wrapped in shawls, a tiny wrinkled creature, with a thin, wailing cry, she raised her arms with an effort and held it close to her.

"Will you take her?" she whispered. "I give her to you. My baby; I shall never see her again. Look after her as your own, and if you like, give her your name."

She made an effort to pass the child towards Magda, but it was too heavy for her weakness.

Magda understood what she wanted and taking the baby in her arms, she held it for a moment against her chest, rocking it gently. The crying ceased; the baby opened its eyes for a moment, then closed them again, as if in contentment.

To Magda's Oriental fatalism, it was as though the baby gave a sign of approval to the transaction. She bent down towards the bed.

"I will look after her," she said gently. "I promise. What would you like her called?"

"Carlotta!" The dying woman said the name as though it were a sacred one.

"It was my mother's," she added faintly after a long silence.

Carlotta loved beautiful things, and she loved them possessively. She wanted them for herself, and she knew that she could never own them in her present circumstances.

She kept this part of her nature carefully hidden from Magda.

It was only a part of her, because she could genuinely enjoy the ready wit, the jovial good-fellowship, and the free and easy way of the actors and actresses among whom she worked.

She liked acting so long as it appealed to her imagination. Anything that gave her, as it were, a new guise for herself.

When she had met Norman she was well aware that

here was a man who could change her present mode of living. She knew that he was rich and that in the future was likely to be richer.

It would have surprised both Norman and Magda, however, had they known that Carlotta, thinking of a possible alliance between herself and Norman Melton, imagined that she was conferring a favour upon him.

"I am a Romanoff," she told herself, "and he was only a working man."

She had no appreciation of the fact that he was self-made, only that he had made money.

She was blinded by that golden barrier round Norman; she saw only the gold, not the man who had risen by his own efforts to make it.

She liked being with him, but she would have found it, even if she tried to do so, difficult to see the man apart from his trappings.

To Carlotta, being with Norman meant a Rolls-Royce waiting for her at the stage door, a warm fur rug over her knees. He meant also orchids on her shoulder, the best table in a restaurant, the service of well-trained, unobtrusive servants, perfect food, and expensive wines.

He gave her a feeling of well-being, of luxury and of comfort, so that it was as easy for her to accept his attentions as to enjoy a soft cushion behind her shoulders.

Something in the urgency of his voice disturbed her when he telephoned.

For a moment when she had first lifted the receiver she had thought that he was about to give her bad news; she was relieved when she knew that he wanted nothing more than her company.

Nevertheless, when he had rung off she stood for a moment by the receiver, thinking.

Every instinct in her body told her that Norman was in love with her, although as yet he had said nothing. But she was unprepared, as yet, to give him an answer. She wanted so much for herself, more than Norman could offer, more indeed, than she could even put into words.

Thinking of the man hurrying towards her now, Carlotta knew that she also wanted love.

She had never known it; never experienced that flaming passion which could make a woman forget everything, even ambition and conventionality.

She stretched out her arms in a gesture of yearning. She saw her face reflected across the room in a mirror, her eyes deep with some unknown emotion, her lips red and slightly voluptuous.

Suddenly, so that it startled her, the telephone rang again. She took up the receiver.

"Hullo," she said.

It was Hector who answered her.

"Are you in, Carlotta?" he said needlessly. "Oh, I am so glad, I was frightened you would have gone out. Listen, I have been given two tickets for the Zoo—Fellow's tickets —for this afternoon. Can you come with me? Do say you will, Carlotta."

Carlotta hesitated for a moment. She knew that Norman would arrive within five minutes. She knew, too, that he was anxious, unusually anxious to see her.

Yet, more than anything else she wanted to go out with Hector. They would go on a bus, they would do everything in the cheapest possible way, and yet it would be amusing.

They would laugh because they were young, because it was just fun, unimportant, quite unserious, and fun.

She made up her mind.

"Listen," she said. "I will come but I shall have to come very quickly. I have got someone coming to see me, and if they once get here I shall be caught. Meet me at Charing Cross in ten minutes. I will wait under the clock. Don't be late if you can help it."

"Wear a white carnation and carry the *Financial Times* in case I don't recognise you!" Hector said, laughing, and added: "You're an angel."

He rang off.

Carlotta laughed out loud. She felt she was doing a crazy thing and she didn't care. She thought of Norman; for a moment a look of anxiety came into her eyes.

Then she picked up her hat and coat which were lying on a chair and ran out of the room.

CHAPTER SEVEN

Magda shuffled a pack of cards and dealt them face up-wards in the shape of a circle, setting the Queen of Hearts in the centre.

Leolia Payne, coming into the room, watched her in silence for a moment. Then she said:

"The nine of spades looks ominous, doesn't it?"

Magda arranged the cards in pairs, paused as she came to an ace and answered testily.

"The diamonds are good."

Leolia Payne crossed to the fireplace, moved two of the cats off the arm-chair and sat down. She was used to Magda's habit of telling her fortune by cards whenever something serious was afoot.

She wondered now what it was, but she did not ask. She knew that sooner or later Magda would be unable to keep her anxiety to herself and that full details of what was troubling her would be recounted to her sympathetic ears.

She drew some knitting from the bag she was carrying, and started to work.

"I can't understand it," Magda said anxiously.

Leolia Payne made no reply.

"It doesn't make sense," she continued. "Two Knaves, the Queen of Diamonds, and the eight of Hearts."

She paused.

"You would say that Norman Melton was the King of Clubs, wouldn't you?" Magda asked.

"Why not the Knave?" Leolia suggested.

She knew now why Magda was fortune-telling. The shop was not the trouble, it was Carlotta.

"Do you want Carlotta," she asked, "to marry Norman Melton?"

Magda laid down the cards and, putting her elbows on the small table in front of her, stared at Leolia.

"The cards show trouble—heart trouble."

"For Carlotta?" Leolia asked needlessly.

"I want her to marry Norman—he will make her happy."

"How can you be sure?" Leolia asked. "Carlotta must choose for herself—we are old, we cannot interfere."

"She thinks that she loves Hector."

Leolia was surprised.

"Has she told you?" she asked.

Magda shook her head.

"At present I think she will not admit it to herself, but when he comes, a bird sings in her heart, her eyes are like lamps in a dark room. Is that not love, Leolia, love as we knew it, years ago?"

Leolia was silent.

"He is poor," Magda went on, "poor and absorbed in his work. He sees Carlotta as a sympathetic friend—to him she is a kindly face in a strange city."

"How do you know this, Magda?" Leolia asked sharply.

"I know," Magda replied in her deep voice. "I know, and my heart bleeds for the child I love, the child whom I would protect from suffering and from pain."

Leolia got to her feet.

"Let us pray that you are wrong," she said anxiously.

CHAPTER EIGHT

Honey St. Clair, whose name before she went on the
stage was Marjorie Robinson, called out:

"Come in."

The dressing-room door opened to admit a diminutive
messenger boy carrying a huge basket of roses and lilies
of the valley and a small, compact green box which obviously contained flowers for the shoulder.

"Well, you are a ray of sunshine, Sonny," she said to
the child. "This dressing-room has been looking like the
Sahara for several days. Put the flowers in the corner and
give the box to me."

He did as he was told, and she looked at the label with a
wistful expression before putting it down in front of
Carlotta's looking-glass.

A few moments later there was a sound of footsteps
outside and the door burst open.

"That devil ruined my entrance again," Carlotta said,
coming in and throwing herself down petulantly on a
chair. "It's really getting beyond a joke, Honey. I shall
complain to the manager."

"He won't listen to you, dear," she answered. "He's always frightened of his leading ladies—I have worked with
him before."

Carlotta shrugged her shoulders. Then she saw the
flowers.

"Are these for me?" she asked.

"Oh, no, darling! Haven't you heard? I have picked up
a millionaire myself. He's a charming man, we met at the
Milk Bar in Piccadilly."

Honey made a face at her, then added:

"I'm not really jealous, but I ought to be. It isn't enough
for you just to have a millionaire in tow, he has to be
generous too."

"You speak as though the two things never go together,"
Carlotta said, reading Norman's card with a faint smile on
her lips.

53

"They don't," Honey said. "Most millionaires are so lousily mean that you have to pay their bus fares as well as your own. Why, one man who used to take me out—who was absolutely rolling—never tipped anybody. I used to feel so ashamed that I used to slip sixpence and shillings into the attendants' hands when he wasn't looking—I couldn't bear it."

Carlotta drew out of the green box a large spray of orchids.

"Oh, my!" Honey exclaimed. "Aren't they lovely? It is a good job you have got your silver dress here to-night. They will look marvellous on the shoulder."

Carlotta tried them against the black velvet frock she was wearing on the stage.

"They are lovely," she said. "Yes, Honey, I am a lucky girl, I suppose."

She said the words, however, with no elation and Honey looked at her curiously.

"What's the matter?" she asked. "Don't you like him?"

"Very much," Carlotta answered.

"But you don't love him, I suppose," Honey went on.

Carlotta hesitated.

"I suppose that is the trouble," she said at length. "I don't love him."

"Good heavens!" Honey said. "You aren't asking much, are you? A millionaire, a good-looking one at that, someone who is generous and makes a fuss of you, an unmarried man into the bargain!

"You are complaining because you want to feel your heart palpitating as though he were some sheik from the desert. Oh, you make me sick! You're greedy. That's the whole point—just greedy. I wish I had your chances."

She applied a stick of grease paint vigorously to her already crimson mouth.

Carlotta looked at her, then laughed.

"You are a sentimental fool yourself," she said, "so don't pull that stuff on me. Who else would slave to keep an invalid husband in comfort at the sea, while you share the cheapest 'digs' in London with another girl?"

"Oh, shut up!" Honey said anxiously. "Don't talk so loud. If it gets known in the theatre about Bill all my glamour will be gone."

Carlotta got up and put an affectionate arm round her shoulders.

"My dear," she said, "your Bill means more to you than

all the millionaires in the world can ever mean to me and you know it."

Pinning Norman's orchids on her shoulder when the show was finished, Carlotta looked at her reflection in the glass and knew that Norman would find her lovely.

The silver shimmer of her lame dress accentuated the smooth magnolia texture of her skin. She drew back her hair from her forehead and from her cheeks, letting it fall in the soft curls at the back of her head.

She clipped onto her ears the tiny pearl-and-diamond earrings that had been a present from Magda on her last birthday. She gave a finishing touch of powder to her nose, and picked up her silver fox cape.

Honey, dressed in a plain black coat and skirt, was waiting for her to go.

"Good night, my poppet," Carlotta said to her. "I wish you were coming with me. It would be much more fun, it would really."

"And what sort of a welcome should I get from the Baronet?" Honey replied. "Carlotta, you look like a dream. If you don't come in tomorrow and say that you have promised to be 'my lady' I shall slap you."

She gave her a quick kiss, then watched Carlotta walk down the stone passage towards the staircase leading to the stage door.

Norman was waiting for her in the Rolls. When he saw her in the doorway he got out and stood bareheaded, his hand outstretched.

"I thought you were never coming," he said.

She knew that his impatience was due to a desire to see her, not because she was late.

She got into the car, letting him put the rug round her legs. She felt dignified as well as luxurious, wrapped in her furs and comfortably seated on the wide soft seat of the car.

She remembered Honey's remark about her princess air and she understood what had been meant.

She knew that with Norman, with all the luxury and extravagance that he could offer her, she became a different person from the laughing, joking Carlotta who hurried in and out of the shabby dressing-room, or went home on a bus with Honey.

Carlotta was peculiarly sensitive to atmosphere. A spray of orchids on her shoulder could transform her into an exotic creature; while at the suggestion of buying a cornet from an ice-cream merchant, she could become a *gamin* child, ready to walk through the streets licking her ice without a thought for appearances.

With Norman she was dignified and quiet. It was, perhaps, his age, or the subconscious respect for his position and money.

She was not sure, she only knew that she found it difficult to be free, either in speech or in manner when she was with him and she often had to force herself to talk at all.

Generally, however, he took the initiative. It was as if he had already prepared what he was going to say and do.

Tonight, as the car drove towards Ciro's Club, he put his hand on hers with a firm touch.

"Are you glad to see me?" he asked.

Carlotta was surprised at the question. It was so unlike Norman to speak in such a way.

"Of course I am," she answered.

He raised her hands to his lips, bending his head so that in the passing light she could see him clearly, noting grey hairs among the dark, and the touches of white on his temples.

"He's old," she told herself.

They arrived at Ciro's and were led to a comfortable sofa-table in the already crowded room. The band was playing, and among the dancers were many well-known, distinguished people.

They bowed and waved to Norman. One or two knew Carlotta by sight and smiled at her as they moved slowly round the floor.

"I hear they have the best cabaret in London," Norman said.

He called for the wine waiter and ordered a bottle of champagne.

Carlotta threw off her cape, touched the flowers on her shoulder, and said:

"I haven't thanked you yet for the orchids. Do you think they look nice?"

He looked, not at the flowers, but at her.

"You look lovely," he said.

His words awakened a memory in her mind of someone else who had spoken them to her, someone who had looked, even as Norman was looking, into her eyes.

Carlotta turned hastily towards an attentive waiter who. was offering her the menu.

56

"What shall I eat?" she asked. "I don't think I am very hungry."

"Nonsense," Norman retorted. "You have had no dinner and you have been working. Let me order you something."

"Yes, please do," she said.

She heard him order an excellent light supper, and thought how nice it was to have someone to make up her mind for her. Perhaps Honey was right, perhaps what she needed was a husband, a man to love her and cherish her.

She thought that she wouldn't mind giving up the stage—indeed it would be a relief. She knew that she would have to work very hard indeed, were she ever to attain fame.

She liked acting and she was quick to sense the right atmosphere, to make any words that she had to say seem natural, and of importance. But she would never be famous. There was no real ambition in her.

She wanted her name in electric lights without the grind and the struggle which were necessary to get them there.

The music, the murmur of the voices, the soft lights and the sparkle of golden champagne in her glass made her feel, at the moment, that this was indeed the better part of life.

"What else can I want?" Carlotta asked herself, for some dissatisfied voice within her warned her that it was not enough.

"Talk to me," she said to Norman quickly. "Tell me what you have been doing."

"I have been in Melchester all day," he answered. "I only got to London at half-past ten."

"How are the works?" Carlotta asked, speaking of them as if they were a pet animal.

"The new factory is nearly ready," he replied. "We have been working on it night and day."

"Are you pleased with the result?" she inquired indifferently.

"I shan't begin to be pleased," Norman answered, "until the machines are going and the aeroplanes are being turned out."

He spoke casually, but into his eyes there came the glowing light of interest.

"How he loves his work," Carlotta thought to herself. "I wish I felt the same way about something."

She sighed, and Norman said quickly:

"You aren't worried about anything, are you?"

Carlotta nodded.

"Yes," she said. "I am worried about myself."

"But why?" he asked.

"I seem to be drifting," she said. "You are always planning ahead, working for the future, looking forward, striving, struggling, full of ambition, and what is more you have the chance of satisfying it. I don't know what I want, and like a child, I shan't be happy until I get it."

"But your acting?" Norman said.

"I could give it up tomorrow," Carlotta answered, "and not notice that it had gone. I like the life, to a certain extent, and the players—they're kindly, generous souls at heart, and so very different from what they appear from the other side of the footlights. But, if I did give up the stage, what else is there for me to do?

"Magda doesn't want me in the business, she never has. I should be quite useless, I haven't her artistic sense or any of her powers of coping with people. No, there seems to be no niche for me. Is it, perhaps, because I am only half English?"

"I think there might be another reason," Norman said.

"What's that?" Carlotta asked.

"That you want a home of your own," he answered.

She started at his words. She realised that he was looking at her as he spoke. She kept her eyes on the dancers.

All at once she had a sense of panic. Norman was going to ask her to marry him and she did not know the answer. In a flash it came to her, all the advantages he could offer.

She could not pretend, even to herself, that she would not like to have a title.

She knew that many social doors would be opened to her, that she could indulge her love of luxury, her desire for travel, the generosity she had always wanted to express, all of this could be hers! . . .

Yet the same warning voice within her added: "And Norman with it!"

She knew that he was going to speak again. That in a moment she must make a decision, one way or another.

She reached out towards her glass, held it tightly between her fingers, raising it to her lips.

As she did so she knew that her hand was trembling and that she was afraid.

CHAPTER NINE

Skye threw herself down on the heather which bordered the lochside, and the two spaniels which had accompanied her on her walk, having quenched their thirst, lay down at her feet.

She had walked for nearly two hours and she felt pleasantly tired.

The backs of her legs ached a little, as they were wont to do after she had been in London for nearly three months without strenuous exercise.

It was a perfect May day. The sky was blue with a few small white clouds blowing in from the sea, and the hills stretching upwards and onwards until they were silhouetted against the blue, were dark with the burnings of last year and green with the promise of new heather.

The small loch, beside which Skye was sitting, was in a cleft high on the hill, and from it a small burn trickled its way down the valley towards the salmon river.

There were many birds at the lochside, for it had been a dry season. The salmon-fishers were complaining, but Skye was content to enjoy the sunshine and forgo the sport. She liked fishing, but this year her grandfather had let his boat on the river.

He could make better use of the rent it brought in. It was the usual state of affairs at Glenholme; Skye could never remember when there had not been talk of poverty and of money.

The moor had been bad in recent seasons and they had been unable to find a tenant for it last autumn. Lord Brora did not mind leasing the moor because he was too old to shoot over dogs and he found it, even with the aid of a pony, too much for him.

But he enjoyed fishing, and he had complained angrily when he had accepted the very good offer which was made him for the fishing at the beginning of the season.

Skye, therefore, found him in no pleasant mood when she arrived for a visit.

It was one of the times when he had a grudge against the Government; the new Income Tax had made him feel more than usually hard up this year, and he raged loudly throughout most meals, glad to find someone who must listen to him.

Skye gave him very little sympathy.

"You have got to pay, Grandpa," she said, "so why not pay and be pleasant? No amount of grumbling is going to help you, and, after all, it is for rearmament."

"Damned nonsense," the old man said. "Who is going to fight the British Empire? That's what I would like to know."

Skye knew better than to be involved in an argument. She tried to turn his attention to herself, or to the estate, but both were unfortunate subjects.

The estate wanted money spent on it, and she herself was a subject of contention in that she preferred to live in London rather than spend the whole year at the Castle.

She had been glad to escape after an unusually stormy breakfast this morning and to get away on to the hills. With the clear air blowing on her face she found that sense of freedom and of homecoming, which she always experienced at Glenholme.

The dogs were wildly enthusiastic at her return. There was no need to whistle for them as she started on her walk, for they were already at her heels, fearful of letting her out of their sight even for a moment.

She climbed up behind the house, went over the top of the moor which directly backed it, then, turning west, moved along the summit until she dropped down towards the small loch which had been her favourite picnic place as a small child.

She was hot and the loch, sheltered by the surrounding moors, was cool and inviting. It took her but a few moments to slip off her brogues, to pull her short green jumper over her head and to unbuckle her kilt . . .

Naked she walked slowly into the water. She gasped at its coldness as it first closed round her knees, rising higher as she advanced until it reached her waist.

Then she struck out. The sun sparkling on the soft, peaty water, dazzled her eyes as she swam; she half-closed her eyes so that she seemed to be moving in a golden haze.

Her body, almost numb from the cold, felt like marble,

but she knew that the moment she came out of the water it would tingle exhilaratingly.

She swam the whole length of the loch and back again, then ran to where the spaniels stood sentinel over her clothes. They barked joyfully as she approached, and she shook herself even as they might have done.

As she had expected, she felt the warm blood flowing back to the surface of her skin. She was so happy that she laughed out loud, talking to the dogs, as she tried, rather ineffectively, to rub herself dry with her handkerchief.

The sun was warm and she swung her arms and legs to make them dry quickly. Then she lay for some moments on the heather, feeling the radiance and the warmth of the sunshine on her bare body.

"This is perfect," she said out loud.

She did not wait too long before she dressed again. As she was doing up her shoes she glanced up to see, to her surprise, a man approaching the loch from the opposite direction to which she had come herself.

She was angry at the thought that he might have come a few minutes earlier and surprised her.

As he drew nearer, she got to her feet and walked towards him.

"You're trespassing, you know," she said firmly, when within earshot. "Who are you?"

He was a tall man and she had to look up to speak to him. When she had spoken, she thought for a moment that his face was vaguely familiar, but she knew all the tenants on her grandfather's estate and could not place him.

"My father sent me up to Burra Hill," he answered. "There's a trap there which requires emptying."

He talked in a quiet, educated voice, so that Skye, still bewildered, asked:

"Your father—who are you?"

"I am Hector McCleod," the man answered.

"McCleod's son?" Skye said. "But, of course, how stupid of me to forget you! How are you, Hector? I haven't seen you since you were a little boy."

She held out her hand.

"It would have been surprising if you had remembered me," Hector said. "I was fifteen, I think, when I gaffed a fish for you in the Withy Pool."

"I remember it so well," Skye answered. "It was my

first salmon, I don't think I have ever been so excited in my life."

They talked of the incident. McCleod had been gillying Lord Brora and Skye had been sent down the river with young Hector as an escort, to try her luck at an easy pool where she would not have to wade.

She had hooked a salmon. It was a big one and it had taken her nearly an hour to play him, until, tired out, he had been coaxed into shallow water and had been gaffed by Hector.

Both children had been wildly excited and Lord Brora had been proud of his granddaughter's achievement.

Skye had not seen Hector since that occasion. McCleod had two other sons, both of whom worked on the estate, and she had often encountered these on her visits to the Castle, but not Hector.

It was shortly afterwards that her mother had married Norman Melton and they spent a great deal of their time in London.

When she was older and had come back to Glenholme more frequently, she had been told that Hector had gone away to Edinburgh and his homecomings had not coincided with hers.

Mrs. McCleod was very proud of the achievements of her third son. Skye always paid a visit to the keeper's wife the second or third day after she arrived at the Castle.

They lived in a cottage by the kennels, and Mrs. McCleod had once been housemaid at the Castle. While in service she had learnt to cook so well that her home-made scones and pastries were the admiration of the whole neighbourhood.

Skye would take tea in the small, overcrowded parlour, while Mrs. McCleod chattered away, telling her all the local gossip, and recounting proudly Hector's prowess.

Skye remembered now that the last time she had taken tea with Mrs. McCleod she had been told that Hector was going to London.

"I must congratulate you on getting your Edinburgh degree," she said. "And I hear you are working for your London one."

"I was lucky enough to have a small sum of money left me," he answered. "My uncle—I'm called Hector after him—died and left me his savings. I particularly want to

62

specialise in bacteriology so I am using my legacy to keep me until I have passed my examinations."

"Well, I wish you luck," Skye said.

She was interested in this boy of whom she had heard so much. She would never have recognised him again; he had altered completely from the untidy, tousle-headed youth who had run to gaff her fish.

She could see little resemblance between him and the old, bearded man who was his father, or the shy, red-faced youths who were his brothers.

The fact that he had lost a great deal of his accent accentuated the difference, for old McCleod was so Scotch in his speech that it was often difficult for strangers to understand him.

Skye turned towards Burra Hill and walked beside Hector.

"Tell me how you like London," she asked.

"I am enjoying the work."

"And you have made many friends there?" Skye questioned.

"One or two," he replied.

He did not volunteer much information about himself, but they started talking of other things, of medicine, of people, and of psychology. Hector had taken psychology among other subjects when working for his Edinburgh degree, and he was amazed to find that Skye knew a good deal on the subject.

"It interests me," she told him. "I have been reading about it and I have attended several lectures in London."

"I thought you went in for painting?" he said.

"I try to," Skye said, "but I shall never be any good. There are thousands of people better than I am and now-adays you have to be first-class at a subject or give it up."

"That sounds rather a harsh judgment," Hector said.

"But isn't it true?" Skye said. "Everything is profes-sional these days. In the past if one had a talent one made the most of it and enthusiastic amateurs got a certain amount of appreciation and made, I imagine, a certain amount of money.

"But today, whether it is in sport or work, people only want the very best, and if I cannot be first-class, I suppose I must look for some other medium of expression."

Hector burst out laughing. She looked at him in sur-prise, and then he checked himself.

"I am sorry," he apologised. "I didn't mean to laugh."

"Tell me the joke," Skye said.

Hector got red in the face. It showed through the brown of his sunburnt skin.

"It . . . was just that you sounded so serious," he said lamely, "and . . . somehow, you don't look serious, if you know what I mean."

Skye knew quite well what he meant. A number of men had said the same thing to her, expressing themselves more eloquently and a great deal more fluently, but with the same idea at the back of their minds.

She appeared too pretty, too small, and too feminine to have any mission in life except the pleasing of men.

For the first time since she had started to talk to Hector she realised that in going away from Glenholme he had altered, not only in appearance and speech, but to herself.

Hector's father and brothers addressed her as 'Miss', they spoke deferentially as befitted a servant of the estate speaking to the laird's granddaughter.

She had been speaking with Hector as though they were equal and thinking of him as such.

It was only when he came to the point of paying her a compliment, that he remembered that she might consider it an impertinence, and had changed the words from those that had been on the tip of his tongue to others less frank.

She looked up at him and knew that he compared very favourably with the men that she knew and who were her friends in London. He was good-looking and he wore his old clothes with an unself-conscious, easy air.

She saw too, that he had an alert intelligence and an expression of determination which comes from hard work and inbred ability.

She made up her mind in that moment how the conversation was to continue, and she killed the shyness between them with a smile.

"If you think I am too pretty to have brains, why not say so?" she asked.

Her remark was deliberately provocative. Hector understood that she was accepting the new relationship between them.

"I have never questioned the fact that pretty women have brains," he answered, "but whether they should have careers or not is debatable."

"Are you still so old-fashioned in your outlook towards women?" Skye asked.

"No, but I am sensible," he answered. "From a theoretical point of view it may be all right for women to claim equality; medically and scientifically it is impossible."

They stopped walking to argue and, still talking, sat down on the heather.

When Hector had got over the fact that he was arguing with a woman, he realised that he would need all his intelligence if he were to justify his arguments. Skye was a formidable opponent.

They talked for nearly an hour before either of them realised it. Finally they turned once again towards Burra Hill.

"Your trouble is," Skye said aggressively as they went on, "that you are going entirely by what you have learnt, not what you have experienced. You are only quoting what other people have discovered, not what you have known and judged for yourself."

"One is bound to do that to a certain extent," Hector answered hotly.

"But why?" Skye asked. "As far as inanimate objects are concerned, yes, but when it comes to human beings, I consider that opinions culled from books are useless. Statistics without the human touch are only waste paper. All the greatest diagnosticians have been psychologists."

"Isn't that rather a sweeping statement?" Hector asked.

"Disprove it," Skye challenged him.

Suddenly they both laughed.

They looked at each other and went on laughing.

"It is funny when you think of it," Skye said. "The last thing I expected when I came out for a walk this morning was to have a discussion of this sort."

"You don't imagine there are many people in the village I can talk to like this?" Hector asked.

"So even the poor, despised female gets a compliment occasionally," Skye said.

They had reached Burra Hill and she looked at her watch to find it was nearly one o'clock.

"I shall be late for luncheon," she said. "Good-bye, Hector, and thank you for a most interesting and instructive morning."

She held out her hand, then as he took it, said impulsively:

"I shall be at the loch tomorrow, if you can think of any further arguments."

She started to run down the hill, through the heather,

before he could answer her. She felt instinctively that he was standing looking after her, but she did not look back.

Only as she reached the Castle did she realise how impossible it would be to explain to her grandfather how she had spent the morning.

She felt it even more difficult to explain to herself how greatly she was looking forward to the morrow.

She decided to say nothing about it.

CHAPTER TEN

Murdoe McCleod stood at the head of his table and said grace.

"Lord, Bless the victuals on this our table and keep peace in our house, Amen."

He sat down and looked expectantly towards his wife as she cut deeply into the golden-brown crust of a big pie. On either side of him sat his sons, Euan on his right, Alan on his left; Hector beside his mother.

It was when he looked at his youngest son that there was a faint gleam of appreciation in the old man's expression. He was proud that one of his boys had not been content to follow in his own footsteps.

He liked, though he had battled against it, the independence which Hector had shown even as a small boy.

Although he had done his utmost to prevent his son from leaving home, from taking up the medical career on which he had set his heart, now that he had gone so far and had already achieved something, his father was proud of him.

It was Mrs. McCleod who had worked in her son's interests, who had taken part in the long, wordy arguments which had gone on for over a year, and it was she who felt, when Hector had gone, as though part of herself had been torn from her.

She loved Hector the best of all her children, and it was her husband who thought most frequently of the little grave in the cemetery where lay the last of their family, Jeannie, who had died a few hours after she was born.

Murdoe McCleod had wanted a daughter. His wife had been content with her sons, and it seemed to her as though the youngest one was all hers, having little of the gravity of his father in him, being from the first a cheerful, vivacious, smiling baby, who had a way with him.

The two elder boys grew up to be eminently worthy. They were respected in the village, but they were shy and made few friends, preferring to spend all their energies in work and asking for no other relaxation than a pipe by the fireside.

Hector was different. He wanted books as soon as he was old enough to read. He was keenly interested in everybody and everything and he had a gift of attending to a sick animal or an ailing child even before he left school.

It was the local doctor who first put the idea into his parents' heads that perhaps, one day, Hector might want to take a degree. He stopped his car when motoring up the strath one day, to talk to McCleod.

The old keeper was coming off the hill, a gun under his arm and two retrievers at his heels. He saluted the doctor

"Guid morning to ye, Doctor," he said. "Is it Mrs. McTavish you are after seeing? I ken she is powerful ill this winter."

"I am going up to her now," the doctor said. "I am doubtful if she will see the spring, McCleod, she's an ill woman. But it was your boy I was going to speak to you about. He came to see me yesterday at the surgery, bringing me a patient."

"Is it Hector ye are meaning?" Murdoe McCleod asked.

The doctor smiled.

"Of course," he answered. "That boy's a born doctor. If you let him throw his gifts away it will be a crime. He brought me in a child who got cut badly on the shore. He had made a tourniquet for him, and done it very well, too. He helped me while I put the stitches in and made himself as useful as any young student might have done in a hospital. You had better save your money, McCleod, for you will have to send him to Edinburgh sooner or later."

The doctor slipped in his gear and started off again leaving McCleod staring after him until the car was far out of sight.

That night Murdoe McCleod told his wife what the doctor had said and added:

"When I see that mon again I will thank him not to be putting ideas into the lad's head. This place has been guid enough for me and for my father before me, and it will be guid enough for him."

Mrs. McCleod had said little at the time, but she had thought the doctor's suggestion over carefully and then spoken to Hector.

She found that the boy had already discussed the possibilities with the doctor himself and that his mind was made up.

It was another two years before things really came to a head. Then Hector informed his father that he must go to Edinburgh. Feelings ran high in the McCleod household.

The two elder brothers were not exactly jealous of Hector, but they felt that it was ridiculous for him to give up a job that was certain for one that was problematical and for which he must spend several years in training, during which time he would be earning no money.

Lord Brora had always employed the McCleod family, and as for various other families on the estate, a place would always be found for the rising generation of McCleods.

The pay was not good; indeed, in recent years it had been very small; nevertheless, there was the comfort of living at home, the contentment of being among familiar surroundings and familiar people.

"Even if you pass your examinations, Hector," his brothers said to him, "do you think you will get a practice?"

That was a question he was asked continually by his family and he always gave them the same reply:

"I know I will."

He spoke neither stubbornly nor defiantly, just confidently sure in the knowledge of his own ability to succeed.

Almost in spite of himself, his father was impressed, but it was to his mother that Hector spoke most freely.

"I have to go, Mother," he said. "I can't stay here. There's something within me which tells me that I am wasting time. I know that I shall succeed; I know that I shall win through."

But for all their pleading Murdoe McCleod would not give Hector the money. He had it—for he had been a careful man all his life, saving ever since he was married against some emergency which never came.

But finally, when it seemed that they were up against a brick wall, when his father would not relent, when his mother could help him no more, it was the doctor who came to his aid.

He wasted no time in beseeching Murdoe McCleod to change his mind, instead he told him frankly that he believed in Hector, he was prepared to back his opinion that the boy would make good and that if Murdoe could not afford to send him, he would make a public collection in the village.

The pride of Murdoe McCleod would not stand for charity. He capitulated, and two months later Hector left Glenholme for Edinburgh.

It was just before he was passing his finals that he received the news that his mother's brother, who was also his godfather, had died and left him three hundred pounds.

To begin with he could scarcely believe his good fortune. Then he realised what this unexpected windfall would mean to him.

At mealtimes with the family gathered round the big white-clothed table, it was Hector who talked. He had, even as a small boy, chattered unceasingly while he ate; in fact one of his earliest remembrances was of his father bellowing insistently from the end of the table:

"Eat your food, lad, and shut your mouth."

The command had never worried him, for even when he was tiny the huge, bearded man had never inspired any fear in him, unlike his older brothers, who sank, invariably, into an awkward silence in their father's presence.

For her youngest son Mrs. McCleod cooked and baked, taking unusual care over the food and loading the table with great plates of floury baps, golden drop scones and crisp, home-made bread.

She noted anxiously that Hector was much thinner since he had been away and she tried, in the few days of his homecoming, to feed him up and make him as well-covered with flesh and as muscular as her older sons.

Their meal finished, Murdoe McCleod took his gun from the corner where he had left it, whistled to the dogs who were waiting for him outside, started off once again up the hill.

There were vermin to be watched for at this time of year, stoats, rats and foxes which might disturb the sitting grouse and destroy the eggs.

The two older boys were working up at the Castle; they got on their bicycles and were soon out of sight, up the narrow track which led to the stables and garages of Glenholme.

Hector pushed back his chair reflectively from the table.

"I wish I could take you to London with me, Mother,"

he said. "I could do with a meal of this sort at least twice a day when I am working."

"I wish I could come with you, son," she answered.

She piled high the dishes preparatory to taking them into the small scullery for washing up.

"One day you shall come," he said, "and you shall see all the sights. The Tower of London, the Houses of Parliament, and the Mint. I will take you round them all."

"That will be fine," Mrs. McCleod spoke with enthusiasm.

She had spent all her life in the village of Glenholme, but she longed to travel, to go South, to see the great cities of which she had heard so much, and of which she was vastly suspicious.

"Are you quite sure they air your sheets?" she had asked Hector, soon after he had arrived on this, his first visit from London.

He had laughed at her, knowing quite well that if he told her the truth she would worry herself incessantly as to his well-being.

He knew how horrified she would be at the small, dingy lodging-house where he stayed; the bedroom, always badly dusted and often left uncleaned altogether; the torn linoleum on the floor; the insanitary little bathroom which was sadly in need of repairs and new enamel.

The spotlessness of his home delighted him.

The linen on the beds, which, though coarse, was spotless, and which smelt of the lavender bags which lay between the sheets when not in use; the lace curtains fresh from his mother's iron; the boards of the floor scrubbed and polished by hand so that there was no speck of dust on them, were all luxuries to which he was not accustomed.

But more than his bodily comforts, he gloried in the freshness of the air, the wind blowing his old kilt round his legs, the rain on his face, and, permeating all, the smell of sea, heather and of pine trees, mingled together.

He got up from the table, put his arm round his mother's waist and gave her an affectionate hug.

"I am glad to be home," he said, and he kissed her cheek.

"And I was thinking that you might be so taken up with your fine friends that you would forget all about us," his mother said, half-jokingly.

But there was a hint of seriousness in her tone, which told Hector that the fear had been there.

71

"Then you are a silly old woman," he answered. "You know I have no time for fine friends."

"No girls?" his mother asked.

As his quick denial sprang to his lips, he checked it, remembering Carlotta.

"I have one friend," he said slowly. "I will tell you about her sometime."

"Do you love her?" his mother asked anxiously.

There was in her voice, as she asked the question, a suspicion of that jealousy which every mother feels when she knows that her son is ready to let another woman take her place in his heart.

For such men as Hector there is room for only one woman, and their first love, which is mother, must inevitably give way for the woman who will be wife.

Hector's laugh reassured her.

"You are an incurable romantic," he said. "No, I am not in love. My heart is in the Highlands."

Kissing his mother again he passed through the doorway of the croft and out into the sunshine.

She looked after him with tears in her eyes. He was so very dear, so very lovable, this son of hers who had been the one person in the family to give her that demonstration of affection for which her temperament had always craved.

Her husband was a quiet, grave man. He loved her in his own way and she knew it, but he never expressed his affection, and his two elder sons took after him.

They had never clung to her, never hungered for her with that overflowing love which must express itself by touch.

Only Hector had wanted her to show her love and had shown his both in deeds and words. He had always made her happy.

As she went about her washing-up in the small scullery, Hector's mother was singing.

Hector wandered out down the narrow garden path, bent down to pick himself a small bunch of primroses, and thrust them into his buttonhole.

Then he struck off towards the river, crossing the fields which lay between the McCleod croft to the woods which, lying down in the strath, made a protection for the stream at that point.

On either side of the river a path had been beaten down by the continual passage of fishermen and shepherds.

It made walking easy and Hector, emerging from the wood, came by way of it to the deep rocky pool known as Pulpits Point.

He sat down and watched the dark, peaty water swirling past, hearing every now and again the splash and swell of some fish rising.

The movement of the water seemed to release in his mind thoughts and feelings which had lain dormant over the past days.

They came creeping down upon him now, questions which required an answer, plans for the future, thoughts of his work and of his family, and memories, vividly colourful, of Carlotta's uplifted face, of Skye's red mouth and blue eyes as she drew him into argument.

At the thought of Skye, other imaginings vanished. He found himself planning what he would say to her when next they met. There was something provocative about her, she stimulated him mentally, she excited his brain.

He wanted to see her again; wanted to talk to her; he wanted to prove himself the victor, the conqueror in their verbal warfare . . .

For the last three mornings they had met on the hill. Today she had not been free; guests were arriving at the Castle.

She had thought it unlikely that she would be able to come to the loch which they had made their trysting-place. Nevertheless, he had waited for her all the morning. She had not come.

He was disappointed, so disappointed that he had been surprised at his own feelings.

He had told himself that it did not matter, that he could sit in the heather, thinking while he waited, but he found himself unable to concentrate on anything, save the path by which she would come.

The hours of the morning had gone by slowly. When it was one o'clock he realised that he had waited in vain.

Now by the riverside he asked himself if it were wise to let such an association continue.

Skye was the Earl's granddaughter, his place was that of a respectful servant. He told himself that there was no reason to think that she had even remembered that he might be waiting for her.

Angrily he told himself that he was a fool, then looking up, he saw Skye coming towards him through the trees . . .

CHAPTER ELEVEN

It was very quiet in the shadow of the pine trees.

A red squirrel scampered along a branch. Skye and Hector lay on the moss-covered ground and talked.

Skye had made her apologies for her absence during the morning.

"Some friends of my grandfather's arrived," she said; "they were motoring and so we were uncertain what time to expect them, and, of course, they came just as I was leaving the house. I had to play hostess. They are both old and rather dull, and, I am glad to say, wanted to spend a quiet afternoon writing letters. I couldn't have been more pleased to escape when luncheon was over."

"What made you come this way?" Hector asked.

"I was going to your house," Skye said. "I thought there was every chance of my missing you, but you might have told your mother in which direction you were going."

Hector looked at her in surprise. He did not say anything, but Skye understood.

"Would it have mattered?" she asked.

"No," he answered quickly. "Of course not."

They both knew that Mrs. McCleod would have thought it strange.

For a moment there was a tense silence.

"Hector," Skye said suddenly. "Do you mind meeting me like this?"

She faced him frankly, her eyes raised to his face.

"It is not a question of my minding," he answered.

"You know what I mean," she said impatiently. "I can't put it into words."

He sat up, looking into the river below them.

"Is it wise," he asked, "from your point of view?"

"I don't know what you mean by that," Skye said. "You are being elusive with me. I want you to be my friend."

"I can't be," Hector answered.

Skye made a gesture of impatience.

"Is there any place in the world," she asked, "so hide-bound as Scotland?"

"It is not a question of being hidebound," he said. "It is a question of our relative positions in life, and you know it."

She laughed.

"And what is the position?" she asked. "You are a doctor and I believe they are accepted in the very best society; I am an unsuccessful artist living in a Chelsea studio."

"And my father," Hector said grimly, "is keeper to your grandfather. Don't you see that friendship between us is impossible, an impertinence on my part which you should properly rebuke?"

Skye got to her feet.

"You are ridiculous," she said sharply. "Ridiculous, and in many ways a fool."

She turned to walk away, but she did not take the intended steps, for Hector also got to his feet and was standing beside her. She half regretted her impulse of anger and turned back towards him.

"Do you want me to go?"

Hector was staring at her.

"Want?" he said hoarsely. "Is it likely that I should want that?"

Their eyes met. They stood staring at each other.

Slowly Hector raised his arms. He put them round Skye, drawing her closer to him. She was trembling and she drew in her breath with a faintly audible sound.

He drew her nearer and nearer, then, like a tempest that cannot be controlled, like the breaking of a torrential storm, he clasped her fiercely and bent his head to kiss her.

The blood was pounding in his ears. He knew no reason, save that he was propelled by a force greater than himself.

She was so small, so tiny in the fastness of his hold. He felt the softness of her mouth beneath his, her hands against his chest.

There was a moment of ecstasy, of joy, as though they fused together in a unity of body and thought, beyond all words, beyond understanding . . .

Hector took his arms away from her and gave a sound which was half groan, half a cry of distress.

Skye, however, made no movement to leave his side. She

steadied herself against him, and stood looking up at his face.

"I love . . . you," she said tremulously, and her voice was very low and soft.

"Oh, my God!" Hector whispered beneath his breath. "What have I done?"

She smiled at him and his distress.

"Don't you understand?" he said, both his hands on her shoulders. "Don't you understand that this is madness?"

"I love . . . you," she said again.

Her words seemed to fire Hector. He drew her close to him again. Yet, when he would have kissed her, he controlled himself; instead holding her cradled in his arms.

He looked down at her lovely flushed face.

"My little love," he said tenderly.

He tried to talk, tried to argue, but he could not. The beauty of the girl looking up at him, the softness of her hands as she raised them to his cheeks, the scent of her hair, and touch of her lips, made him aflame with a madness which forgot everything, save that he might kiss her again and again.

He closed her eyes with kisses, he bent back her head and kissed her on the neck, on the tops of her small, rosy-lobed ears.

"Tell . . . me," she said in a whisper. "Say it to . . . me, Hector."

"I love you, I worship you."

His voice was deep with emotion.

It seemed a long time later that they drew apart. They were both transfigured by their emotion. Skye's face was alight with a happiness which seemed in its intensity not of this world.

She held out her hand in an eager confiding gesture. Hector gripped it fiercely.

"We have got to talk," he said seriously. "Don't look at me, my darling, I can't bear it if you do."

"Don't let us talk," she tempted him. "Words spoil everything, let us just be happy, let us forget everything but ourselves and our love."

He shook his head.

Skye sighed. But it was a sigh of contentment rather than of distress.

"All right," she said. "You can talk first, but I know all your arguments and I don't agree with any of them."

"Darling," he pleaded, "don't make it more difficult."

"I am not," she answered. "I know exactly what you are going to say, that we must give each other up, never meet again. Isn't that it?"

Hector nodded miserably.

"Well, I am sorry," Skye went on, "but I refuse to be abandoned by you or any other man that I love. I love you and you love me . . . you do . . . don't you?"

There was just a touch of anxiety in her last question. Hector turned himself round to face her, and putting his hand beneath her chin, looked straight into her eyes.

"Listen," he said. "Whatever I say to you, whatever I suggest, it is because I love you. Because I realise now that from the moment I saw you that morning by the loch, you have never been out of my thoughts or out of my heart. I was afraid to face the truth in myself afterwards, but I love you, I think I have always loved you, and I know that I always shall."

He bent forward and kissed her. For a moment they clung together again. Then he put her sternly from him.

"That doesn't mean that we can go on seeing each other," he said, "that we can be together."

"But it does mean . . . that," Skye cried.

Hector was silent for a moment, then he said:

"Are you suggesting that I should walk up to the Castle, see your grandfather, say to him:

" 'I love your granddaughter, Skye.'

"He would say to me:

" 'Who are you?'

"And I would answer:

" 'I am the poor man at your gate, the son of your keeper, the third generation of men who have touched their caps, taken your bounty and been in your service.'

"What do you think your grandfather would say?"

"What do you think he would say if I came to him and said: 'I am in love with a doctor. He's a man called McCleod. You have never heard of him because he comes from a different part of Scotland'?"

"That would be easier," Hector admitted truthfully, "but I don't come from a different part of Scotland. I come from Glenholme. I have been born here, reared here. I have attended the village school, and my mother waited on your mother, wearing a cap and apron as a badge of office."

"Then what do you suggest that we do?" Skye asked in a very small voice.

"I suggest," Hector answered, "that you go away and forget me, that you go back to the life to which you belong and perhaps sometimes, you will remember, when you come along this river, that you had a moment's happiness with a man who has passed out of your life."

"You are a coward," Skye said.

Hector started at the word.

"I'm not," he answered, then added brokenly: "Oh, my dear, do you think this is easy to do?"

"Of course it isn't," Skye answered. "It is impossible. That is why we aren't going to do it."

She put out her hand again and took his.

"We're two clever, intelligent people," she said firmly. "We both know what we want, we both know exactly what we intend to get from life. Are we going to let a bygone tradition, the opinions of a few harmless people, really hinder us? Of course we aren't."

She looked up at him with a smile.

"Hector McCleod," she said, "I ask you to marry me."

"No!" he snapped at her violently.

"You will," she said. "You have got to . . . I will make . . . you."

She spoke as furiously as he had and for a moment they glared at each other.

Then she was in his arms once again. He was kissing her and holding her to him as though he would never let her go . . .

It was getting late when finally they walked towards the Castle. The dying sun cast a crimson glow on the red trunks of the pine trees.

The first evening star trembled and glittered in the deepening shadows of the sky. Hector held Skye's hand tightly as they walked together. They were quiet now, for at last even words had failed them.

They had talked and argued and they had come to no conclusion. They only knew one thing, beyond all words, beyond all possible contradiction, that they loved each other with a fire and a passion which could not be denied.

"I am only here for three more days," Hector told her.

They had come to a gate in the woods which led into the Castle grounds.

"I am coming back to London in a week," she said.

"It doesn't help," Hector said. "Don't you understand, darling, that I can't take you out in London. I have got no money, at least only enough to see me through my examination—if I pass it quickly."

"There's one thing I won't stand," Skye said, "and that is talk about money. I have got a little, a very little, and what we have we share together. I will listen to your arguments for a time, at any rate, about our love and our marriage, but if you are going to be proud and absurd about my paying for myself, I shall go raving mad."

Hector laughed, he could not help it.

"There are so many difficulties," he said.

"They aren't going to matter," Skye replied.

Then she put her arms up to him and drew his head down to hers.

"And now good night . . . my dear love . . . my own . . . darling," she whispered.

He held her closer.

"Good night," he said. "What time shall I see you tomorrow?"

"I will be at the loch just as early as I possibly can, about half-past nine or ten, perhaps. Oh, Hector, it's a long time to wait, isn't it?"

She clung to him, then with a sudden movement, wrenched herself away.

"I must go," she said. "God bless you."

She opened the iron gate and slipped through it. She started to run through the trees, turning before she was out of sight to blow him a kiss.

He watched her, he closed the iron gate through which she had passed. It seemed to him symbolic of all that lay between them. She was inside the Castle grounds, he was outside.

For a long time he stood there. All his doubts and perplexities seemed to hedge him round, encompass him like evil spirits which would not be exorcized.

He knew that into his life had come something so miraculous and so wonderful that he hardly dared to contemplate it.

This was love, as he had always dreamt of it; this was the reason why he had never cared for other women, never been interested in the girls of the village who had done their best to make him notice them before he went away.

In Edinburgh he had met women with the other students. They had shown him quite openly that they liked him and wished to further the acquaintance.

But always he had forgotten them; had failed to take

79

advantage of the advances they had made; he preferred to have his friendships with men, or to be alone.

He knew now that this had all been a prologue for the coming of Skye. He knew that in his heart he knelt down before her, as a priest might kneel at a holy shrine.

He wanted her passionately; he loved her with a fire which would not be denied, but, at the same time, passion was but a small part of his love for her.

It was for her sake that he was afraid; it was for her sake that he felt the only decent course for him to pursue was to leave her alone.

She must not be hurt, must be protected from the hardness of life, from everything which was not perfect and beautiful . . .

Hector had never been in the slightest ashamed of his family or his birth.

He had made no secret about the men with whom he worked, and, indeed, in Edinburgh it was the usual thing to find clever and successful men coming from the poorest homes.

With anyone else in the whole world he was prepared to hold his head high, to demand from them the respect due to his manhood, regardless of his social position.

But with Skye it was different. She was the unattainable.

He made a sound in his throat. It was almost a sob. 'Unattainable'—the word repeated itself in his mind.

With slow steps, his head bent, he walked slowly back the way they had come, towards the lights of his father's croft.

CHAPTER TWELVE

Two days later Skye faced her grandfather, standing defiantly before the old man who was sitting in a high-backed oak arm-chair beside the hearth.

"Where did you meet this man?" Lord Brora asked.

"Has that got anything to do with it?" Skye questioned.

"Will you, or will you not, answer my question?" her grandfather stormed.

"You haven't answered mine yet," Skye told him.

The old man snorted.

"The whole thing is preposterous. I think you must have taken leave of your senses."

"I expected you would say something like that," Skye said to him. "Whenever the older generation cannot understand the modern outlook, they always say we are mad."

She spoke coolly, her voice raised a little, for her grandfather was slightly deaf.

"But you can't marry the son of my keeper," Lord Brora said in more modified tones.

"Why not?" Skye asked. "He's a clever young man who will go far."

"And where will you stay when you come to Glenholme?" her grandfather said. "At the Castle or down at the McCleods'?"

"We shall be delighted to come here, if you will have us," Skye said.

"Do you imagine that I would accept that young jackanapes in my home?" Lord Brora thundered. "Coming here after my granddaughter—the damned impertinence of it!"

"Grandfather!" Skye put a restraining hand on his arm. "Listen to me a moment. I love Hector McCleod and he loves me."

"Love! What's love got to do with it?" her grandfather inquired. "The man's not of your class and you know it!"

Skye went a little nearer the old man's chair. Then she said:

"Will you please tell me something, Grandfather, and tell me honestly. Why did you let my mother marry Norman Melton?"

Lord Brora stared at her under bushy eyebrows and did not answer.

"You approved of that marriage, didn't you?" Skye went on. "I believe you encouraged it. Will you tell me why?"

"He was a decent chap," Lord Brora growled.

"And a rich one," Skye insisted, "very rich, but at the same time he was the son of a Melchester labourer! He went to work in a factory when he was a boy. He certainly wasn't of my mother's class—and you know it!"

"It was an entirely different position," Lord Brora said.

"Different because Norman had money. That was the only difference," Skye answered. "If Hector was a millionaire you would be delighted for me to marry him—and you know it!"

"Good God! McCleod's my keeper, his wife was housemaid here in the house. Do you expect me to welcome their offspring as my granddaughter's husband? I won't have it, I forbid it. You aren't to marry this man. That is my last word."

"And if I do?" Skye asked.

"You needn't come here again," Lord Brora said.

"Very well," Skye replied, "that is quite plain."

"And what is more," he said as she turned away, "you can tell the young man that his father can clear out of the cottage the day he marries you. I will not employ him or his two sons on the estate."

"Grandfather" Skye exclaimed. "You can't mean that. You can't mean that you would turn out McCleod! Why, he's lived at the cottage for sixty years and his father was there before him, with your father."

"If you marry his son, he goes," Lord Brora said.

Skye went up to her grandfather and touched his arm.

"Do you really mean that?" she asked him.

"Of course I mean it," he said. "I don't usually say things I don't mean."

"It's the most damnably unjust, the most unfair thing I have ever heard."

"Well, you can take your choice," he replied, "but that is my decision and I shall not change it."

Skye knew that the old man meant what he said. She stared at him for a moment, wondering if she could make one more appeal to his generosity, but she knew it was hopeless.

Lord Brora was an obstinate man and a hard man. He was a good landlord and kind, but as a magistrate he was known for his strong convictions and his merciless judgments.

Poachers and vagrants in the neighbourhood were terrified of him. He would give them justice, and he was never unfair, but when he convicted he gave the maximum sentence without pity and without mercy.

Skye walked out of the study door, slamming it behind her. For some moments Lord Brora remained seated at the fireplace.

Then he rose to his feet and squared his tired shoulders. The interview had exhausted him, but he was quite unperturbed by Skye's defiance.

"She will come to her senses," he said aloud. "The impertinence of the fellow!"

He rang the bell and waited for some time before the old butler, who was nearly as old as he was and who had grown grey in the service of the Castle, came to the door.

"I want to see McCleod," Lord Brora told him.

"Who, my lord?" the butler came nearer, for he was growing deaf.

"McCleod, the keeper. Have him sent for. He's to come to the Castle as soon as he gets home."

"Very good, my lord."

Skye was waiting outside in the hall as he came out of the study.

"Who did he ask for, Masters?" she said

"McCleod, Miss Skye. His lordship wants to see Murdoe McCleod."

"I thought so!" Skye said.

She ran out of the house and down the garden path towards the river. It took her nearly ten minutes of fast walking to reach the McCleods' cottage. When she got there, panting a little, she saw Euan working in the garden.

"Is Hector here?" she asked, over the fence.

Euan McCleod looked up in surprise. He had not heard Skye approach. When he saw who it was he raised his finger to his forehead.

"Guid morning, Miss Skye," he said. "I will find Hector. I don't think he's awake yet."

He put down his fork and went slowly into the house. Skye waited.

A moment later Mrs. McCleod appeared, wiping her hands on her apron.

"Good morning, Miss Skye," she called. "Is it Hector you want to see?"

She was obviously surprised at the request and doubtful if Euan could have brought the right message.

"Yes. Is he in the house?" Skye asked.

"He's at the back, getting some wood for the fires," Mrs. McCleod said. "Won't you come in, Miss Skye, and sit down."

"I won't, thank you," Skye answered. "I want to have a word with Hector and he can walk back with me along the river."

Mrs. McCleod was obviously flustered at all this. She started pulling down the sleeves of her white blouse, which were rolled above the elbow while she cooked.

"Is his lordship keeping well, Miss Skye?" she inquired.

"He is very well, thank you," Skye answered. "And your family—how are they?"

"We are awful pleased to have Hector with us," Mrs. McCleod replied, "and the boys are always well, thank the Lord. But McCleod's been suffering with the rheumatics again this past fortnight."

"I am sorry," Skye said.

She saw Hector in the doorway.

"Miss Skye wants to speak to you, Hector," Mrs. McCleod said, pushing him forward.

Skye went towards him.

"Come down by the river," she said, in a low voice. "I want to speak to you. Good-bye, Mrs. McCleod, I am sorry to have bothered you."

She and Hector walked away together while Mrs. McCleod stood staring after them, an anxious expression on her face.

"What does Miss Skye want with our Hector?" Euan asked from the doorway.

Mrs. McCleod started.

"She didna say," she answered shortly and went back into her kitchen.

Skye told Hector what had occurred.

"I came to find you at once," she said, "so that you can tell your father before Grandfather speaks to him. Have you said anything yet?"

84

Hector shook his head.

"Nothing," he answered.

"Then you must," Skye said. "You must tell him at once."

"What do you expect him to do?" he said in a hard voice. "Pack his box and leave the house where he has lived all his life, give up his job!"

"No, no," Skye said, "of course I don't want him to do that. Grandfather will change his mind—I will make him. It is tyranny, it is a wicked, cruel threat to force me to give you up."

They had reached the shelter of the pine trees. They stopped and stood staring at each other.

"What are we to do?" Hector asked and his voice was low.

Skye put her hand into his.

"Fight!" she said. "We will fight and we will win."

Hector kept her hand but he made no effort to draw her farther into his arms.

"I can't let my father and my mother suffer," he said. "You see that, don't you?"

"Of course I do," Skye answered gently.

"I told you," Hector said miserably, "that it was impossible. Now you see my words are being proved true."

"And afterwards," Skye said, "you told me that you loved me, also you promised to marry me, Hector."

"You made me say it," he said. "I've tried to save you from yourself and failed. I knew, you see, that this would be the outcome of any attempt to approach your grandfather.

"Do you think that if there had been the slightest chance that he would allow me to marry you, I would not have gone to him myself? But how could I? The son of the keeper, who, at a moment's notice, without the slightest regard to years of service, he can dismiss from his employment."

"Hector," Skye said gently. "Do you still love me?"

He looked at her with misery in his eyes. Then he reached out his arms and drew her close to him.

"I adore you," he said.

There was no fire in his voice, only the broken tones of one who faces the end of all happiness.

"Do you love me," Skye insisted, "more than your sense of propriety, more than your respect for tradition and convention?"

"Why do you ask?" Hector said, puzzled.

"Answer me," Skye commanded, "answer that question —now."

"I love you more than anything in the world," Hector said. "You are mine and I am yours."

"Very well, then," Skye said. "That's all I wanted to know. I have got a plan—a plan which will make everything come right in the end, but you have got to agree to it."

She put her arms round his neck and drew his face nearer to hers.

"Kiss me first," she said, "before I tell you. I am a little afraid of you."

"My darling!" he said.

His lips met hers. The kiss which started gravely and as a solemn expression of their love, kindled them both into a rapture of joy and passion.

They clung together. It seemed to Skye as though time stood still . . .

She knew only that this love that she felt for Hector enveloped her completely. She became his, she was a part of him.

She knew beyond all argument, beyond all reasoning that such a love one for the other must in the end conquer all things.

It was impossible that the world could separate them, keep them from each other.

She felt now that from the beginning, some power greater than themselves had intended a union between herself and Hector.

There might be arguments, there might be difficulties, but sooner or later they must be smoothed away and conquered because it was right and indisputable that he and she should be one person.

She loved him. This was what she had been waiting for all her life; all that she had wanted. This satisfied her emotions, her desires of something fuller than the social round.

All those yearnings for herself and for the future were centred now in another. She had found the career she had sought so long, in Hector and his love.

In attending to him, in making him the apex of her life, she could create something fine, something strong and of real importance.

At present, Hector could not see things as she did. He

was afraid, not for himself but for her. He doubted the wisdom of their love, even while he could not deny its omnipotence and the overpowering strength of their emotion.

He wanted her with all his heart and with all his soul. Skye believed in him, she knew that there was for him a great future.

He was not so far-sighted. His modesty, his humility, forbade him to see things as she saw them. But there was within him a deep faith and that faith would never fail him.

As their kiss ended Skye put her cheek against his and gave a little shuddering sigh of relief and contentment.

"Does anything matter," she whispered, "but this?"

For the moment he was content to look into her face, to echo her radiance, and believe, with her, that this moment was eternal and nothing else mattered.

"You can't give me up," Skye told him.

The shadows of worry and anxiety came into his eyes again, deadening the joy and ecstasy.

"Shall I go and see your grandfather?" he asked.

Skye shook her head.

"No," she answered, "it would do no good. I want you to get hold of your father, before he goes to the Castle, and tell him to agree that marriage between us is impossible. Persuade him to tell my grandfather that he will oppose it with all his might."

Hector stared at Skye in amazement.

"I thought . . ." he said.

Then he checked himself.

"You are right," he said in a dull voice, "marriage between us is impossible. It's what I have told you, and at last you have come to see it."

Skye looked at him, at the misery on his face, at the hopeless despondency, which seemed to shatter for the moment even his virility and strength.

Then she laughed.

"Darling," she said, "you are awfully stupid about some things, even though I do think you are the cleverest man in the world."

"What do you mean?" Hector asked.

"Listen to me," she said. "Your father must go to the Castle and do as I say. The two old men will agree together that the whole idea is preposterous, mad and ridiculous. You and I will go back to London tomorrow."

Hector shook his head.

"We can't get married quietly," he said, "if that's what you are thinking about. You know, as well as I do, that the press would find it out. Then your grandfather would fulfil his threat and turn my father and mother out of the cottage."

"I am not suggesting that we should get married," Skye said. "I am going back to London with you, Hector McCleod, and I shall live with you in open sin."

Hector stared at Skye as though she had gone mad. A deep flush crept slowly up his face.

"You will do nothing of the kind," he said.

"But I will," Skye answered. "Don't you understand, darling, it is the one thing which will bring them to their knees. I won't marry you, but I will live with you as your wife. I am not ashamed to do it. I shall be glad and proud to be your mistress, under any circumstances."

"I refuse," Hector said violently.

"Darling, you told me that you loved me more than convention, and yet, the first time I ask you to be unconventional . . ."

"I love you too much to shame you," Hector said.

"You are being very Scotch," Skye replied, "and very traditional. It is the one possible chance for us and for our happiness. You know it is."

"I won't do it," Hector said stubbornly.

"Why not?" Skye asked. "Answer me that question, quite honestly."

"I will tell you," Hector said.

He suddenly knelt at her feet, taking both her hands in his.

"I worship you," he said very gently. "To me you are perfect, the woman I have always dreamed about, the woman I never thought I would meet. If you imagine that I could touch you in any way that was not the most beautiful, the most holy . . ."

Skye felt the tears springing into her eyes.

"My dear love," she said. "My dear stupid, beloved, wonderful Hector. I will live with you in the same house and we will let the old people believe what they see.

"We will force their hands, we will make them give their consent to our marriage, but, between ourselves, everything shall be exactly as you want it. Our love is strong enough to keep us pure until we can be married."

Then she bent and kissed his lips.

CHAPTER THIRTEEN

Carlotta waited for Norman in the lounge of the Ritz Hotel. They had arranged to have luncheon together.

She had accepted the invitation more because it had afforded her an avenue of escape the night before, than because she was really anxious to see him again.

She had managed to stave off his proposal of marriage, but only by artificial means which made her feel cheap and insincere.

"I refuse to talk seriously," she had said at Ciro's Club. "You look serious this evening, and I feel all sorts of ponderous statements are coming from you. Forget them, let's be gay, let's be happy and irresponsible."

Norman had a sixth sense in an approach to a deal.

It had stood him in good stead in the past, and now it helped him to control his impatience which urged him to continue, to find out, once and for all, Carlotta's feelings towards him.

He had tried for weeks to find the right moment, to get her in the right mood, to discover if her interest in him went deeper than the acceptance of his company at luncheon and supper.

He did not realise, or he would not face it, that Carlotta was avoiding the very moment for which he was looking. Last night she had escaped by pretending, at first irresponsibility and afterwards exhaustion.

All the time they were at Ciro's she had managed to keep up an unceasing burble of small-talk. She had made him dance, she had made him laugh, and she had gone out of her way to greet numerous acquaintances.

People whom, on other occasions, she would have passed by with a wave of the hand or a friendly smile, she welcomed as though they were her dearest friends.

She was sparkling and radiant and her good spirits were infectious. But when finally the bill was paid, the cabaret over and the restaurant emptying, Carlotta got into Norman's car and sank wearily back against the soft cushions.

"I'm dead," she said. "It has been a lovely evening, but now I've got a headache. Don't talk to me, let me just relax until we get home."

She looked very beautiful in the dim light; her eyes closed, her pink-tipped fingers dropped limply in her lap. Norman wanted to take her hands, to hold and to kiss them, then to draw her close into his arms.

Instead, he stared steadily out of the window, his arms crossed, his mouth set in a determined line.

When they stopped at the shop, Carlotta opened her eyes.

"Are we back already?" she said. "I am so sleepy. Don't get out, Norman dear. I am sure you are tired too."

He did not obey her but stepped out of the car first to help her alight. When he would have come with her into the shadows of the great doorway, she stopped him.

"I will find my own way upstairs," she said. "Good night, and thank you for a lovely evening."

"Carlotta!" Norman said hoarsely.

It was a cry of a man driven almost beyond his strength. She relented.

"I must see you tomorrow," she said. "Will you telephone me in the morning?"

"Lunch with me," he said pleadingly. "I shall be in London. I can be free by half-past one, if you will meet me at the Ritz, or anywhere you like."

Carlotta had another engagement but her conscience was pricking her for her behaviour during the evening.

"I should love to," she answered. "The Ritz—one-thirty."

Blowing him a kiss she opened the door and closed it sharply behind her.

Only when she was alone in her bedroom, watching her reflection in the mirror as she raised her hands to unpin the orchids from her shoulder, did she look herself honestly in the eye and say:

"I am in love with Hector."

Until that moment she had never dared face the truth. Now she could pretend no longer. She liked Norman, she admired him, and she enjoyed all the attention he gave her, but he aroused within her no passionate response.

Hector, the man she had seen but a few times, of whom she knew so little, was the man to whom she had given her heart.

Something deep within her, which she had never suspected, was thrilled by the thought of his lean, strong body, by his clever face, with his young, visionary eyes. Hector gave her the impression that within him was a dynamo of power that was driving him forwards and onwards, towards his ideals.

That, she felt, was perhaps the difference between the younger man and Norman. Norman also was dynamic, but he was materialistic—a realist, he would say.

There was about Hector the indescribable glow of a man who is always looking at the stars and sees that the road ahead of him is only worth studying because it leads to them.

But he had nothing else—no position, no money, only a problematical future.

"I am crazy," Carlotta told herself, "crazy, but I can't help it."

This past week since Hector had been away, she had felt as though something vital had gone from her life. She had attributed it to restlessness; she had refused to face the truth.

But now she could no longer deny her own heart. She wanted Hector; wanted to see him again, to hear his voice, to know that thrilling, unexpected shyness which his presence always brought to her.

He would be back in London the following day and she knew that was the reason why she had staved off the proposal of marriage which had been trembling on Norman's lips tonight.

"What am I to do?" she asked herself.

She sank down on the chair before her dressing-table and buried her face in her hands. It seemed to her that she stood at a crossroads.

On one side there was Norman with wealth and position; on the other, Hector, penniless—his only asset his confidence in himself.

"I'm a fool, a damned fool," Carlotta said.

She flung herself face downwards on her bed and started to cry.

She had not cried for years, and all the pent-up excitement of the past weeks, the accumulation of fear, of doubt, and of anxiety, were culminated in this moment of self-revelation.

When she had awoken in the morning, she told herself how silly she had been to worry and be upset. But as the sun came streaming in at her bedroom windows, she knew that the day was glorious because Hector would be back in London.

She expected him to telephone her. The morning passed without the bell ringing. Only as she was leaving for the Ritz did the boy come hurrying to tell her she was wanted.

With a cry she ran towards the instrument.

"Hullo," she said, and her voice was pregnant with anticipation.

"I am speaking for Sir Norman Melton," a man said.

"Oh," Carlotta ejaculated. After a pause she added: "Miss Lenshovski speaking."

"Sir Norman may be a few minutes late for luncheon, Miss, he has been kept."

"That's all right," Carlotta replied. "Tell him I will wait."

She put down the receiver with a bang. She was bitterly disappointed but she excused Hector to herself.

'I expect he's kept at the hospital,' she thought. 'He will ring me this afternoon, or before I go to the theatre. He will know that I want to see him. He must know that.'

Magda was already eating before Carlotta left.

"I am lunching with Norman," Carlotta said, pulling on her long black gloves.

"Where?"

"At the Ritz, darling."

Magda glanced up at her with knowing eyes.

"You are looking pale," she said. "Something has upset you, what is it?"

Carlotta shook her head.

"Nothing," she replied. "I expect it is too many late nights. I didn't get in until after two."

"Was that Hector on the telephone?" Magda inquired casually.

At the unexpected question Carlotta felt the warm blood in her cheeks. She turned away, but not before Magda had seen the blush.

"No," Carlotta said. "Is he back?"

Magda didn't waste words. She merely looked at her adopted daughter, and with a shrug of her shoulders went back to her food.

When Carlotta had gone, she went slowly down the passage towards Leolia Payne's room, and sitting down at her bedside, for she was laid up with a cold, she talked to her for nearly an hour.

Carlotta's feelings for Magda were those of irritation as

she drove towards the Ritz. She wanted to keep the secret of her love for Hector hidden.

"But I might have known," she told herself, "that Magda would find out."

It was the first time in her life that she had deliberately kept anything from the old woman. Always they had discussed the men who loved her.

It had been, though Carlotta did not realise it, her safeguard which protected her far more ably than any constant chaperonage could have done.

Magda with her understanding of people, with her gift of finding the truth in every man, however skillfully it was concealed, could guide Carlotta, prevent her from forming wrong impressions, or giving her affections where they would not be valued.

But this, Carlotta told herself passionately, was a secret she would share with no one, not yet, not until Hector had confessed his love to her.

That he would not love her was something which never entered her head. She was so certain that it was only his shyness and his inexperience of women that prevented the admiration she had seen in his eyes growing into something deeper and more tender.

She had laughed gently to herself at the moments when he had turned away from her, moments when he had only to lift his hands, and she would have been in his arms.

"I want him," she told herself, yet for the moment she could not formulate any plan.

She only knew that this unknown emotion, surging within her, made her desire Hector as she had never deemed it possible that she would desire any man.

Love to Carlotta had always been something which other people felt for her; they had roused little response in her and she had been content to be admired, always the one who took, never the one who gave.

But now, this radiant tempest made her feel as though she was reaching out towards all the world. She wanted to transmit her inner happiness to others, to infuse them with her own joy.

When she reached the Ritz she did not mind waiting for Norman. She was content to sit in one of the red-plush arm-chairs and watch the fashionable crowd passing to and fro.

The band was playing a soft, sentimental waltz. Carlotta felt as though she were upon a stage. It was all so luxurious, so unreal, this sophisticated social life of which she had, as yet, but touched the fringe.

'This world could be mine, if I marry Norman.'

The thought came to her, it tempted her.

She saw herself, not as she was, an unknown actress, but as a person of importance.

She could come here as 'Lady Melton', entertain and be entertained by some of the distinguished and famous people who now passed her by without a second glance.

The pearls round her neck would be real; there would be diamonds glittering on her wrists; a Rolls-Royce waiting outside to carry her away when luncheon was over.

'I should be somebody,' Carlotta whispered to herself. 'I should not have to work, only enjoy myself.'

It seemed to her she hesitated before an enticing shop-window.

She watched Norman come through the swing doors, give his hat and stick to a liveried attendant and look round the crowded foyer for her. She waved her hand.

"Forgive me for being late," he said as he approached her.

Carlotta knew at once that something had upset him. His mouth was set in a grim line, his eyes were like steel. He did not offer Carlotta a cocktail.

"Shall we go in?" he asked abruptly.

Surprised, but without argument, she led the way towards the restaurant. A table had been kept for Norman in the window and they were bowed to it by attentive waiters. They ordered their meal.

"What's the matter?" Carlotta asked as soon as they were alone.

"Why should you think anything is wrong?" Norman questioned.

"I can tell if you are upset," she smiled at him.

He looked pleased, the grimness of his face relaxed.

"That is very sweet of you."

"You are a funny person, Norman," Carlotta said. "On first acquaintance you seem a strong, silent business man, the type one meets in books or on the stage. I felt at first as though nothing could upset you, nothing disturb your air of calm efficiency.

"If the roof fell in, or a fire broke out under the table, I believed you would cope with it and emerge unruffled, still calm, reserved and unsurprised. Now I still feel you could cope with anything, but I have grown to know that you are vulnerable all the same."

"Carlotta," Norman said, bending forward, "you could help me so tremendously in my life, if you would."

He had not intended to propose to Carlotta in such a manner. He had planned so many things he might say.

Now the words came from him, just in the course of conversation so easily, so unsensationally, that he might have been asking her any commonplace question.

Carlotta lifted her eyes to his, then glanced away quickly.

"I want you to marry me," Norman said quietly. "I think you know that. I think you must have known it for a long time. I love you more than I can tell you.

"I am not good at expressing myself, but I love you, Carlotta. I would make you happy—at least I would do everything in my power to see that you were."

"I don't know," Carlotta said in a low voice. "I don't know what to say."

With an effort she looked at him.

"To be honest," she said, "I knew that you loved me. There is no reason otherwise why you should have troubled about me so much, should have taken me out, telephoned me, continually sent me flowers.

"You have been very kind, Norman, and very patient, but the awful thing is that it isn't getting us very much farther. I don't know what to say to you."

"Let me make up your mind for you," he suggested.

"How I wish you could, but it isn't as easy as all that."

"Isn't it?" he questioned. "Say 'yes', Carlotta, say you will marry me and I will arrange everything. We can wait a little while, if you like, and then we can go away on our honeymoon. When we come back, Belgrave Square will be ready for us. You can come up to Melchester and see my house there—I think you will like it. There are people I want you to meet, people who will make a great fuss of you because you are my wife."

He paused, then added:

". . . and who will love you because you are yourself, because you are so beautiful."

"I don't know," Carlotta said miserably. "Oh, Norman, how difficult it is to settle one's own life."

"And if you were helping someone else, what would you advise her to do?"

"I would say she was a fool not to marry you," she answered. "You are clever, Norman, and you are rich. Oh, yes, I am not pretending that money isn't important, because it is, but you are always so kind and so terribly nice. Any girl would be a fool to refuse you."

"Then don't be a fool," Norman suggested.

"I can't decide like this," Carlotta said. "Give me time to think, Norman. Don't hurry me."

"You shall have all the time you want," he answered gently.

Just for a moment, he let his hand rest on hers as it lay on the table.

"I want things to be as you wish," he said. "Only remember that I love you and don't make it too hard for me."

"I won't," she promised.

"We must drink to the future."

Norman called the waiter. Opening the wine list he chose a bottle of champagne and ordered it to be put on ice.

Carlotta sent away her untouched plate of food and asked if she might have a cigarette.

"I can't eat," she confessed.

Norman bent forward with a lighted match.

"You aren't to be worried," he commanded.

"That's easier said than done," Carlotta smiled at him. "And talking about being worried, tell me now about yourself. What had upset you when you arrived here?"

"I had a very difficult interview with my stepdaughter," he replied, "and I am afraid I lost my temper. It isn't a thing I often do, especially with Skye."

"What has she done to annoy you?" Carlotta asked in surprise.

She had heard a lot about Skye and she knew how fond he was of his wife's child.

"I don't know whether I ought to tell you," Norman said, "but I know that you will respect my confidence. Perhaps one day we shall have no secrets from each other."

"Tell me," she said curiously. "You know I'd never say a word to anyone."

"Well, Skye has fallen in love," Norman said, "and unfortunately she has chosen for the object of her affections, the son of her grandfather's keeper. The family has been employed on Lord Brora's estate for two or three generations. They are ordinary, hard-working, decent people.

"The son, however, in whom Skye is interested, has left

his home and taken up a career for himself. They met and apparently immediately fell in love with each other.

"She went to her grandfather and informed him that she wanted to marry the man. Lord Brora was, not unnaturally, furious, and has forbidden her to do anything of the sort, threatening that if she does so, he will turn the keeper and all his family off the estate."

"How unfair!" Carlotta interposed.

"I suppose he thinks that it is just an infatuation, which will die away under a certain amount of opposition. With most people, I expect that would have been the result, but unfortunately, Skye is both obstinate and tenacious when she wants something. She is determined to have the young man and will allow nothing to stand in her way."

"But surely he can't allow his family to starve?" Carlotta asked.

"No, he quite appreciates that fact, which makes matters worse."

"Why?"

"Lord Brora having forbidden the marriage," Norman answered, "Skye left Scotland and came to see me this morning, having just arrived off the train. She told me that she and the young man have arranged to live together until such time as her grandfather should see sense."

"Good Heavens!" Carlotta gasped. "But what will Lord Brora do?"

"I can't imagine," Norman answered. "He's as obstinate in his own way as Skye is in hers."

"But you can't let her do that, surely?"

"Let her!" Norman ejaculated. "I argued, I threatened, I pleaded with her, none of which had any effect. She loves this young man and she intends, I gather, sooner or later, to be his wife. I can do nothing."

"Poor Norman," Carlotta said.

She was well aware how much this would upset him.

"I've done everything I could do to dissuade her—everything," Norman said. "By the way, I believe you have met the man. I have heard you mention him, I think."

Carlotta turned and stared at him. She felt as if an icy hand gripped her heart, as though the blood was drained away from her face, leaving her deathly pale.

"I mentioned him?" she exclaimed in a faint voice. "What is his name?"

It seemed to her that the whole room receded from her,

that everything round her became misty and indistinct; clearly, almost loudly, she heard Norman's voice answer her:

"He is called McCleod—Hector McCleod."

CHAPTER FOURTEEN

Skye clambered up the step-ladder and fixed the pleated frill of brightly-coloured chintz to the pelmet boards above the casement window.

She was humming as she worked. In the pocket of the overall which covered her dress were a large business-like hammer and a workman-like pair of scissors.

An outside door slammed, vibrating through the tiny room. A moment later Hector came in.

"Darling!" Skye exclaimed. "You are early, how lovely."

"I got away as soon as I could," he replied, "and just managed to catch the right bus. You know it is an invariable rule that it leaves one minute before you get to the stop."

She turned to clamber down the steps, but he lifted her from the second step into his arms.

He kissed her passionately, her mouth, her eyes and cheeks, then, holding her at arm's length, he said:

"Let me look at you. Yes, you look really domesticated. A perfect wife for a tired business man."

"How did you get on in the laboratory today?" she asked.

"The chief was delighted with me," he answered. "I showed him my experiments in the last week, and I got a special commendation, in front of the whole class. Oh yes, you can be proud of me, I deserve it."

"A little praise goes to your head," Skye said severely. "Come and look at what I have been doing. It is far more important than any amount of bugs."

She showed him the curtains she had made and already hung.

"You are clever," he told her. "I don't believe anyone else could manage to make such a show for sixpence halfpenny, or is it sevenpence we spent this week?"

"It is a good deal more than that," Skye answered, "but after all it is worth it. This is our home."

"Will be," he corrected, taking up her hand and kissing it.

They had taken the flat in Victoria after two days' long search, walking, as an exhausted Skye said, some millions of miles before they were satisfied.

Finally, in an old courtyard, they had found what they sought. Originally the rooms over a coach-house, they reached them by climbing a small iron staircase, which some previous tenant had painted green.

Beneath them the old stables had become a garage, used by the tenants of a modern building recently erected near by.

The flat itself enchanted them. There was plenty of light and air, and except when the cars were being taken in and out it was completely quiet.

There was also a tiny flat roof outside the kitchen, which could be converted into a roof garden when they could afford the time and the money.

One large room, with an old fireplace, served as a living-room, and out of it led a large, comfortable bedroom, which at the moment was Skye's alone. Communicating with it was a tiny room, which was Hector's.

The square hall into which the front door opened would serve as a dining-room, and there was a kitchen and a bath-room.

"It is perfect," Skye exclaimed, as soon as they saw it.

A few hours later they had signed the lease and taken over the keys.

Once he had fallen in with Skye's suggestion, Hector lost no time in regrets or anxieties as to the course they were taking.

He believed with her that a love such as they had for each other was more important than anything else, and he knew that to obtain their happiness they must be prepared to brave public opinion.

"Of course I have told Grandfather that I shall tell every-one where I am and what I am doing," Skye said, "but actually we will be discreet at first, hoping that he will come round before we need advertise ourselves too vio-lently!

"I have written him a long letter," she added, stating exactly what we aim to do and telling him that I have seen Norman. He will either come to London himself, or ask Norman to go to Scotland, and between them they may be able to see sense."

"What shall I do if your stepfather comes round and fights me?" Hector had asked.

"Fight him back," Skye replied. "He'll like it, too. He has always taken everything he wanted in the world, regardless of opposition, so he can't expect to stop me."

"He will try!" Hector answered.

"But of course he will," Skye said. "You would, in the same position, wouldn't you?"

"I would kill anyone who treated my stepdaughter as I am treating you," Hector answered.

"If they only knew how respectable you are," she laughed. "It's like being with a maiden aunt."

Hector, indeed, had kept strictly to the rules that he had set himself, when he had first agreed to their living together.

At night he kissed Skye good night, then they both went to their own rooms, not meeting again until breakfast. Under no circumstances would he enter her room once she had retired for the night.

And although Skye laughed at him for his scruples, she respected him because, having chosen for himself a course of action he stuck to it, whatever the temptation to do otherwise.

Today, looking at him as he inspected the improvements she had made in the flat, she thought, as she had done so many times during the past week, how greatly he was improved by happiness.

He looked younger and his face radiated contentment and joy.

Skye was not surprised when he came home with stories of how nice people had been to him, how he had been singled out by his fellows for some attention, or by the doctors for special praise.

She guessed that in the past he had always been too reserved, that he had kept away from his fellow creatures, rather than mixing with them.

Her advent into his life had changed his whole outlook and she was glad that it was so.

"Oh, who do you think has been here today?" she asked.

"I can't think," Hector answered. "Was it a visitor?"

"A most important visitor!" Skye replied. "Norman—my stepfather."

"What did he say?" Hector asked.

"It is just as I expected," Skye answered. "Grandfather has written him pages of fury, and has insisted that he go up to see him in Scotland. Norman got the letter two or three days ago, but he couln't go before, because he has been in Melchester, seeing about the new factory.

"He leaves for Scotland tonight, and has promised to come here as soon as he returns to tell me exactly what Grandfather has decided."

"Was Sir Norman still very angry?" Hector asked.

"He tried to be," Skye answered, "but I soon wheedled him round. In fact, he was so sweet that I simply longed to tell him that things weren't as bad as they seemed."

"Why didn't you?" Hector asked.

"And spoil the whole plot?" Skye exclaimed. "Don't be so silly. What is really worrying Norman and Grandfather is the fact that I might have a baby. That's our strongest card, darling, and we will play it for all we are worth.

"Norman didn't put it so crudely to me, of course, but he talked all round the subject, until finally I said to him:

" 'I suppose the thing that really worries you is the consequence of my sin, rather than the sin itself.' "

"What did he say?" Hector asked.

" 'I trust you have thought of such a possibility.' And I replied, 'Of course, darling, but it takes nine months and, so far, Hector and I have only lived together for six days, so there is plenty of time for you and Grandfather to relent and make the child legitimate.' "

"Your frankness is always a little devastating," Hector said. "Was Sir Norman upset?"

"No, he laughed," Skye confessed, "and I think that he will really try and make Grandfather see sense. After all, Norman can't throw stones at anyone. He started life at fourteen shillings a week."

"And I'm not even earning that," Hector said.

Skye put her arms round his neck.

"Think of all the money you are going to make," she said, "when your patients queue up outside our mansion in Harley Street."

"And if I never get there?" Hector suggested.

"We shall be just as happy in Balham or Wigan," Skye replied.

"I love you," he answered, "I love you."

He pulled her nearer to him, so that he could kiss her neck where the overall opened to reveal a triangle of white skin.

"But listen," Skye protested, freeing herself, "you haven't heard all the excitement yet. Norman's going to be married, and to one of your friends."

"Carlotta," Hector guessed. "I'm glad."

"I do hope I shall like her," Skye said. "Long before you told me about her I begged Norman to be careful. He is such a divine person, really, but he must marry the right woman."

"Carlotta's very sweet," Hector said. "By the way, you know, I feel very guilty not having rung her up. She and Mrs. Lenshovski were very kind to me. I want you to meet them, of course, but I can't spare the time to see anybody. I would so much rather be alone with you."

"Well, I think we shall see Carlotta very soon," Skye answered. "Norman tells me they are being married in a fortnight's time."

"Why so quickly?" Hector asked.

"I can't think, except there's nothing to wait for. Carlotta wants to leave the stage and Norman can only take a short honeymoon, so they might as well get away at once."

"Is he very happy?"

"In seventh heaven," Skye replied. "I have never seen a man so excited—much more excited than you are about me."

"I don't believe it," Hector replied. "It isn't possible!"

He held out his arms, but Skye avoided them.

"I have got work to do," she said severely, clearing away the tea-things.

"Can I help?" he asked.

"When we have been married a few years you won't say that. You will lie back with your feet on the mantel-piece reading the evening paper while I slave around for your comfort.

"Look out, silly," she added hastily, as Hector, tilting back her head to kiss her, very nearly upset the tray that she was holding in her hands.

Laughing and joking in the kitchen they were both startled by the sound of the electric bell buzzing over the front door.

"Who can it be?" Skye asked.

Hector shook his head.

"I have no idea," he answered. "I will answer it."

He went towards the door and a moment later Skye heard him say:

"Yes, she lives here. Won't you come in?"

She peeped round the door to see Mary Glenholme entering.

"Mary, darling!" she called out, and went towards her with outstretched arms.

"Your grandfather gave me your address," Mary said rigidly.

Skye realised with dismay that she had come as an enemy, rather than as a friend.

"I didn't know you would be back in London so soon," Skye said, "otherwise I should have given it to you myself. When I came and fetched my clothes from the studio, they told me that you were not expected home for at least a fortnight."

"I intended, if you remember," Mary said, "to come back at the same time as you did. You went to Glenholme for a month, but I understand that circumstances caused you to return after one week."

Skye waved a hand in the direction of Hector.

"Will you be introduced to the circumstances?" she said. "Hector McCleod, whom I'm living with."

Mary looked at her severely.

"That's not very funny, Skye," she said.

"It's not meant to be," Skye said. "It happens to be the truth."

"But Skye . . ." Mary said.

Hector intervened.

"I know what Lord Brora has told you, Miss Glenholme," he said quietly, "but I think that in justice to Skye and myself, I ought to explain that we want to get married and that Lord Brora, by withholding his consent and by his threats towards my parents, has forced us into this position, one of which I, at any rate, am not proud."

Mary looked at him for some time.

"Explain yourself, young man," she said.

Hector explained more fully, and Skye saw that Mary's rigidity was relaxing.

"It certainly is a very different story from what Lord Brora has written to me," she said.

"Well, what's he said?" Skye questioned. "Do let's see the letter."

"Certainly not," Mary replied. "It would only upset you, or at least, if it didn't, it ought to. I think you are behaving badly, Skye, but what Mr. McCleod has told me does certainly put a different complexion on the matter."

"Good!" Skye said. "You might have guessed Grandfather would have been biased."

"But surely you could have waited?" Mary said. "Why all this haste?"

"Because, darling, we should have got no farther," Skye answered. "You know Grandfather, you know no amount of argument will ever move him. We should just have gone on nagging and nagging, while Hector and I got more and more unhappy. So in the end I thought it best to do things at once, to come here and force his consent. He is bound to give it in the end."

"You are very confident," Mary said.

"Of course I am," Skye replied. "You see, it means everything to me to have Hector."

She slipped her arms through his.

"Give us your blessing, Mary," she coaxed. "I can't bear it when you are cross with me."

"You are hopeless, Skye," Mary replied. "I came here fully prepared for a scene. Incidentally, I meant to take you back with me, but it doesn't look as though I am going to have much success."

"I am afraid not," Hector said with a grin.

"Of course, I am getting blamed for all this," Mary went on. "Your grandfather ascribes the whole thing to my pernicious Bohemian influence."

"Oh darling, what fun!" Skye cried. "If he only knew how respectable your studio was. It is quite the dullest in the whole of Chelsea."

"That doesn't make things any better for me," Mary answered. "Now the whole family will abuse me and one can't blame them."

"Well, the whole family need never know," Skye answered, "if you can persuade Grandfather to see sense. I have told no one but Norman, and although he is furious, I should think it is unlikely that he has advertised his anger to anyone else."

"No, I expect that's true," Mary answered.

"Listen," Skye said. "I have got an idea. Why don't you go up to Glenholme tonight with Norman—Grandfather has sent for him, and if you go with him it would be the best thing possible. You could try and persuade him to see reason."

"There's something in that," Mary said reflectively. "It seems to me that if you two have made up your minds to get married, then you had better get it over."

"You have never spoken a truer word," Skye replied.

"Come on, we will go out and telephone Norman from the call box. We can't afford a telephone here, needless to say."

She snatched up her hat and hurried them down the green staircase, out into the street below. When they reached the red call box, Hector produced two pennies and Skye dialled Norman's number.

"Can I speak to Sir Norman?" she asked.

"Hold on, I will put you through," she was told.

"Norman," she said, when she heard his voice, "Mary's here. She has been an absolute angel about everything and has agreed to go up to Scotland with you tonight and beard Grandfather!"

"That's a good idea," Norman said.

"So, listen, darling," Skye went on. "We will bring her to the station. What time is your train?"

Norman told her he was leaving Euston just before midnight.

"I thought he wouldn't go earlier," she told the others when she joined them outside. "That gives him time to say goodbye to Carlotta. Perhaps she will be at the station too. So at last I shall meet Hector's friend and Norman's fiancée."

"Does Hector know Carlotta Lenshovski?" Mary asked curiously. "How extraordinary. This seems to be a general mix-up. I mean, Hector's father being on your grandfather's estate, Norman marrying an actress who knows Hector."

"I quite agree," Skye interrupted. "It is all frightfully dramatic. Now if only Hector had been married to, or in love with, Carlotta, we should all have been related in one way or another."

"Don't be so absurd," Hector said.

Skye looked at him curiously, struck by a sudden thought.

"I suppose she isn't in love with you, darling?" she asked. "After all, your meeting was very romantic and all that sort of thing, and there is no reason why she should have gone on seeing you so often, is there?"

"I have never heard anyone talk more nonsense, have you?" Hector asked Mary.

"It might quite easily be the truth," Skye answered, but she slipped her hand into Hector's and gave it an affectionate squeeze. "Anyway, you belong to me now, don't you?"

In spite of Mary's presence he put his arm round her shoulders.

"That's one thing of which you can be quite certain," he told her gravely.

CHAPTER FIFTEEN

Carlotta came into the room bearing a parcel in her arms. She put it down on the table in front of Magda.

"A present from the company," she said.

"What is it?" Magda asked, pulling aside the wrappings of tissue paper.

It was a china figure of Mrs. Siddons. Underneath was the inscription:

'To Carlotta Lenshovski, in commemoration of her marriage.'

It was followed by the names of all those who had subscribed to it and who had been acting with Carlotta in the play.

"It is pretty," Magda said. "It was kind of them, wasn't it, my darling?"

Carlotta was standing in front of one of the mirrors on the wall, running her fingers through her hair, which had been flattened by the tight cap of satin and lace which she had been wearing.

Something in her tone and in her expression told Magda that all was not well. She looked at Carlotta anxiously. Tomorrow was her wedding day.

Carlotta had insisted, in spite of all protests from Magda and from Norman, on acting until the very last possible moment.

The management had been willing to release her, but for some reason she wanted to finish with the stage on the Saturday night and become Norman's wife on Sunday morning.

Norman would have been content with a quiet wedding at a registry office, would indeed have preferred it, but some obstinacy in Carlotta had made her refuse to agree to his proposals.

Instead she was determined to be married in church, wearing the traditional white satin and orange blossom.

"I am entitled to it," she said. "I have never been mar-

108

ried before, and I can never be married again with the same fuss and excitement. I will be a conventional bride."

Norman had agreed, as he was only too willing to agree to anything that Carlotta wished. But he had been surprised at her persistence that the wedding should take place so soon.

He was, of course, overjoyed, except that some curious perversity in Carlotta at the moment made her appear to delight in hurting him whenever the opportunity arose.

"Of course, our wedding will mean nothing to you, Norman," she said one day, as plans were being discussed. "I mean, you have been through it before and your vows certainly weren't very successful the first time, were they?"

"This is different," he said gently.

Carlotta with raised eyebrows, retorted:

"I expect you said that to your first wife."

She seemed to delight in bringing, whenever possible, Evelyn's name into the conversation. Norman could not understand her.

However, generously, he attributed it to over-excitement and the agitation which he believed every woman must feel before taking a decisive step into a new life.

But on the Friday before their marriage, she had dispelled any anxiety he might have had in his mind as to her wishes about their marriage.

"I can't believe that in forty-eight hours from now you will be my wife," Norman said in a low voice, as they drove home together from the theatre.

"Are you quite certain you are glad?" Carlotta asked him.

"My dear," Norman answered softly. "I can't believe it is true. Are you quite certain that you want to marry me?"

"Quite certain," Carlotta had answered softly.

He had believed her and the joy which had flooded into his heart made him dedicate anew his life and all his work to her.

Carlotta had, however, refused to see him the day before the wedding.

"I have got too much to do," she said. "You must wait until Sunday, until we meet in the church."

Magda had been surprised at her decision, but she also had learnt not to argue too often with Carlotta these past weeks. Never had she known the girl so easily moved to anger, so petulant, if the slightest difficulty arose.

"Your dress is here," she said now. "I have put it in your bedroom."

"How does it look?" Carlotta asked casually.

"Lovely," Magda answered.

"I was a fool," Carlotta said, coming away from the mirror and sitting down at the table. "I ought to have been married in scarlet, in green, or some sensational colour."

"It wouldn't have suited you as well as white," Magda replied.

"It would have given the newspapers something to talk about."

"Haven't you had enough publicity?" Magda asked, thinking of a stack of press cuttings which had arrived every day since Carlotta's engagement was announced.

She and Norman had been portrayed to the public as figures in some fairy-tale.

The romance of Norman's life story had captured popular imagination and his engagement to a beautiful young actress was just the type of news with which the editors were pleased to feed their public.

"I like to give them something to talk about," Carlotta said.

She spoke with a kind of smiling bitterness, and Magda pushing aside the plate in front of her, leant towards her adopted daughter.

"Tell me the truth, Carlotta," she said. "Why are you marrying him?"

Carlotta raised her head and faced Magda.

"Because he is rich," she said. "Why did you think I was doing it?"

Magda shrugged her shoulders.

"I don't understand you," she said. "I never know if you are telling the truth or if you are acting for me as you act for everyone else. What are your true feelings, child? Make up your mind about them, before it is too late."

"It was too late weeks ago," Carlotta said. "I made up my mind then."

She rose and walked towards the mantelpiece. She stood for some time with her back towards Magda, staring at the ballet shoes in their glass box.

"Are you blaming me?" she asked.

"What for?" Magda asked. "For playing a dangerous game with your own life? Why should I blame you? If I believed you, I might pity you."

110

"And why is it dangerous?" Carlotta asked. "Won't Norman be able to give me everything I have ever wanted?"

"Are you quite certain what that is?" Magda questioned. Carlotta turned round and looked at her.

"What am I to do?" she said, and her voice quivered.

"My darling, my little one," Magda answered. "Isn't it a little late to ask that?"

Carlotta suddenly put up her hands to her head.

"I am mad," she cried. "I feel mad, my brain is aching, I can't see or understand what I am doing. Oh, Magda, you have never failed me before, help me now."

She walked up and down the room. Magda clasped her hands together in agony, longing to help the child that she loved.

"What is it?" she asked. "Explain to me. I may be stupid, but I don't understand."

"I love him," Carlotta moaned. "I love him. I wanted him, but what was I to do?"

"Hector?" Magda asked in a whisper.

"Oh, Magda, Magda."

Carlotta ran across the room to her, and flinging herself on her knees beside her adopted mother, hid her face in her lap.

Magda put her arms across the thin shoulders which were shaking with sobs.

"My little dove," she said, "my little star, don't cry."

"What am I to do? What am I to do?" Carlotta asked.

For some moments Magda allowed her to abandon herself to her grief. Then, stroking the thick, curly hair bowed low on her lap, she said gently:

"Listen to me, Carlotta, I have something to tell you."

With an effort Carlotta controlled her sobs; they grew quieter, the force and tempest spent itself, and although her breath still came in sudden gasps, she was calmer.

"I will tell you something," Magda said. "I will tell you why I was glad when you told me you were to marry Norman. He is rich and I want money for you. You may think it strange that I should say this, when everyone thinks that I also am a rich woman, but it is not true."

Carlotta raised her head in surprise; but her eyes were swollen and red. She stared at Magda through her tears.

"The money I shall leave you will not be a very great sum. You will have a certain amount, of course, but taxes will have to be paid and they will be considerable.

"That was why, when you told me that you were going

to marry Norman, I was glad. At least it was one reason for my gladness, there are others."

"What are they?" Carlotta asked, through dry lips.

"I think that he will be a steadying influence on you," Magda answered. "When I knew your mother, she was an ill woman and you were about to be born, but there was a wildness in her which I could understand, because we were of the same race. I had seen it before, many times, in those of my countrywomen who had played fast and loose with life."

"But what do you mean?" Carlotta asked. "I don't understand."

"Such women lack balance, my darling," Magda said. "They lack a sense of proportion. They concentrate on whatever comes to hand, they do not use their intuitive vision, they will not see beyond their noses."

"That's hardly true in my case," Carlotta said. "I am ambitious, you know I am."

"What for?" Magda asked.

Carlotta hesitated.

"Aren't you just imagining that you are?" Magda suggested. "You want to be rich and important, you want to be noticed, talked about, made much of. Carlotta, my sweet, my lovely child, that is self-satisfaction, it is not ambition?"

"Why isn't it?" Carlotta asked.

"I know, because once I was ambitious. But I am not clever enough to explain to you in words. Ask Norman, he knows. He has true ambition within him."

"And Hector, also?" Carlotta asked.

"Perhaps Hector also has it," Magda replied.

"Why must this happen to me?" Carlotta questioned. "If only Hector could have loved me, things might have been so different."

"He has no money," Magda answered. "Don't you require money, Carlotta? Even as a child you always chose the most expensive things, demanded the best in everything. Would you have been content to be the wife of a struggling doctor, even if in the far-distant future he may become great? There will be many years of struggle first."

"I don't know," Carlotta said. "I only know that I love him."

"I wonder!" Magda replied. "I wonder if you have begun, as yet, to understand the meaning of love. I have known it once, only once in my life. It is still a very lovely

112

dream! My life went on without that ecstasy, without that joy.

"Now, when I am an old woman, I look back over the years that are past, I ask myself if I did not, in fact, feel a deeper love for Ivor. We had companionship, we had an understanding with each other which seems to me to be well worthy of the name of love."

"I want your dream love," Carlotta said. "I want Hector —I want him."

She spoke passionately! After a moment she rose to her feet and going to the side table, took a cigarette out of a box and lit it. Slowly she regained her composure.

"I hate Skye," she said. "I hate her!"

She spoke now in the same firm, hard voice she used earlier in the day.

Magda looked at her with sorrowful eyes.

"It is silly to be jealous," she said.

"Can I help it?" Carlotta questioned furiously.

"She is Norman's stepdaughter," Magda said warningly, "and he is very devoted to her."

"She hates me too," Carlotta answered.

"How do you know?"

"When we met, for the first time, on Euston Station, she knew that I was not in love with Norman. I felt her dislike of me, I knew that she would have done anything in her power to stop the marriage if she could."

"She loves her stepfather," Magda said wisely.

"I don't think she suspected that I cared for Hector," Carlotta went on. "I hardly looked at him although he was so friendly, so damnably eager to introduce me to Skye. He hoped we would be friends—poor fool! Why are men so blind, so unperceptive about women?

"Norman tried, too, to urge Skye and me into friendship. He was ponderous about it and slightly patronizing to both of us.

"At that moment I hated them all. I wanted to run away, Magda, to come back to you, to forget both Hector and Norman as quickly as I could. As the train carried Norman out of the station I waved good-bye. I was left with Hector beside me and Skye watching me with chilly suspicion of me crystallizing into certainty.

"She was telling herself that I was marrying her stepfather for money and I knew that as soon as I had gone, she would be saying so to Hector.

"If I could have killed her there and then I would have

done so. As it was, I smiled politely, said good-bye and came home alone in Norman's car.

"Twice I have seen Skye since then. Norman has insisted on our lunching or dining together, but Hector has not been with her. He's been kept at the hospital, or some such excuse."

Carlotta clasped her hands together.

"Do you think," she said breathlessly, "that he is avoiding me for the reason that he loves me but daren't face the fact?"

"My little dove, don't delude yourself," Magda said gently.

The glow faded from Carlotta's face.

"I know," she said. "I have got to face the truth and tomorrow I have got to face Norman."

"Don't marry him," Magda said gently. "Put it off before it is too late. Telephone him now, say you are ill and later tell him the truth. You are young, you are pretty. Why should you throw yourself away on someone you don't love?"

Carlotta stamped her half-finished cigarette into the ashtray. With a hard, forced laugh, she picked up the china figure of Mrs. Siddons, and looked at it.

" 'To Carlotta Lenshovski, in commemoration of her marriage,' " she read aloud.

"Magda," she said, "I mustn't look back. After all, he is a very rich man."

CHAPTER SIXTEEN

"Dare we go to the wedding?" Skye asked Hector; but when he suggested that she should go without him, she refused.

"No, I must have the courage of my convictions," she said. "It is only that the family *en masse* is rather a bitter pill to swallow at one gulp!"

"You must go," he said. "Your stepfather would be terribly hurt if you weren't there. He is so fond of you."

"He's the sweetest person in the world," Skye answered. "Do you know what he offered me yesterday? An allowance."

"I hope you didn't take it," Hector said quickly.

"Knowing your pride, darling, I refused, but I said that we would be delighted to have it as soon as we were linked in the holy bonds of matrimony!"

"How I wish I could support you myself," Hector said angrily.

"Well, you will be able to, some day," Skye answered, "and in the meantime, it is ridiculous to have any pride about it. I only refused Norman because I realised that his offer was merely a sop to his own conscience.

"He's worried about us living like this and he felt it would ease his mind if we were really comfortably off. As it is, my refusal will make him work all the harder to get Grandfather's consent."

"He is taking a long time to relent," Hector said unhappily.

"Time is a thing which never enters into consideration at Glenholme," Skye replied. "It just drifts past them, taking them gradually nearer the grave, but so peacefully that they don't realise what is happening."

"I want you to be mine," Hector said simply, putting his arms around her.

"And I want you too," Skye replied.

He kissed her and for a moment they both forgot everything else save their passion and desire for each other. Trembling a little Skye moved away from him.

"It is your rules and regulations which are making things so difficult," she said, half-jokingly, half-seriously.

Hector turned her round to face him.

"You aren't regretting anything?" he asked. "If I thought you were troubled, if I thought in any way I was making you unhappy, I would walk out of your life and never come back. I love you enough for that, you know."

She put her fingers over his mouth to stop him speaking.

"Don't be silly," she said very gently. "It is only sometimes that I find it hard to keep on the pedestal you have designed for me. It is very wonderful being adored, my Hector, but at times I feel very human."

"And do you suppose that it is easy for me?" he asked, his voice deepening with emotion.

She smiled at him, knowing that he was finding it very hard. Many nights she heard him walk up and down his tiny bedroom, unable to sleep because she was so near to him, yet divided from her by an impenetrable wall of honour erected by himself.

"I am terribly nervous," she whispered as they knelt side by side in the small grey stone church where Carlotta was being married.

She felt an answering pressure of his hand on hers and knew that he understood.

They had bravely faced the eyes of Skye's relations as they had walked together down the aisle to take their places in the front row, which Norman had reserved for them.

In the same pew was sitting Alice, his sister, and two of Evelyn's cousins.

Alice, who had only seen Skye once in her life, held out her hand, encased tightly in a white kid glove.

"I am so glad to see you again," she whispered. "Do you remember me—I am Norman's sister Alice."

"Of course I do," Skye answered.

She remembered vaguely that her mother had always said scathing things about Norman's sister, finding her dull and unintelligent. But somehow she liked the honest, kindly face of the grey-haired woman, and she realised with a clear perception that she had done her best to look smart for her brother, though her plum-coloured coat and skirt and beige fox fur were in lamentably bad taste.

"I do hope Norman will be very happy," Skye said.

She was surprised to see a sudden rush of tears come into Alice's eyes.

"She is very lucky," Alice answered. "He is so kind and generous."

There was a large congregation to see Norman and Carlotta joined as man and wife. On Carlotta's side there were a number of the theatrical profession and in the front pew Magda and Leolia sat in solitary state.

Skye's relations eyed critically the more flamboyant stage-stars, while the party of Norman's employees who had come up from Melchester picked out their special favourites with much whispering and excitement.

Carlotta had chosen lilies as a decoration for the church and they gave out a heavy, exotic fragrance which seemed, at times, almost overpowering. Norman, entering from the vestry, looked pale and anxious, but Carlotta, who was nearly ten minutes late, was completely composed.

There was a click of cameras, the flash of lights, the whirr of a cinematograph, when she arrived.

The choir burst into song and Carlotta, carrying a huge bouquet of purple orchids, came slowly up the aisle towards her future husband.

Only as she reached the front pew did she raise her eyes as she passed Hector.

She just looked at him then away again, but Magda watching from the other side of the aisle, felt that in that look she had given away her secret to the world.

When the ceremony was over, the bride and bridegroom came down the aisle to the strains of the *Wedding March*. Norman's car was waiting for them and they drove away to Belgrave Square, where there was to be a small reception.

As they got into the car someone in the crowd rushed forward and thrust a bunch of white heather into Carlotta's hands.

"God bless you, dearie," she called out, "and good luck."

Carlotta threw the heather on the floor.

"It is unlucky," she said with a shiver, "for me, at any rate. I never allow it in my dressing-room before a first night."

"Nothing could be unlucky for us now," Norman answered.

He put out his hand to take hers, but she gave a sharp cry.

"Mind my veil," she said. "It tears so easily. You must be careful."

She was smiling and there were two bright pink spots of colour in her cheeks as they shook hands, talked and laughed with their guests at the reception. She had never looked more lovely, but Magda knew she was agitated.

When Carlotta went up to dress before going away she followed her, and finding her alone, shut the door behind her and locked it.

"I want to speak to you for one minute," she said. "I want to wish you every happiness, my darling, and beg you now that you are married, to do your best to make Norman a happy man, to be to him a good wife."

An expression crossed Carlotta's face which seemed to Magda to be one of fear, but it was gone as quickly as it came, and she could not be sure of what she had seen.

"Go away, darling," Carlotta answered lightly. "You will make me cry if you are so sentimental, then all my eyelashes will run and I shall look a freak. I feel exhausted."

Magda was powerless to do anything but obey her.

When she opened the door a crowd of laughing, chattering friends came trooping in and she knew she would never have a moment alone with Carlotta again.

In Norman's room, Skye was sitting on the bed watching him tie his tie.

"I wish it was me," Skye said.

Norman turned round from the dressing-table and came and stood beside her.

"Listen, Skye," he said. "I have got an idea. If the old man won't relent, the only thing for me to do is to give you enough money to support Hector's family. You could get married then."

Skye shook her head.

"It is terribly sweet of you, darling," she said, "but you don't understand. Hector would never accept that, nor would they. They have lived in the place all their lives. They couldn't imagine an existence without work, without the Castle overshadowing their croft as it has always done. They are proud, too, terribly proud. No, we can only wait and hope Grandfather will give in; sooner or later, I am sure he will."

"He's a very obstinate man," Norman said slowly.

"And I am very obstinate too," Skye answered. "I have got youth on my side. I can wait—he can't afford to."

"That's the hardest thing I have ever heard you say," Norman replied.

"Is it?" Skye answered. "I am not really bitter or angry with him. I see his point of view. What he doesn't realise is that the world has changed; that the barriers of society are falling and fading away. To him Hector is a servant, to me he is a man, and that is all that matters. It is the difference of our generation and that difference has got to be fought out between us."

"Well, bless you, my dear," Norman said. "As long as you are happy, I am content, though I wish you could have found some other way."

Skye looked at him with shining eyes.

"It's a question of courage," she said. "You would have done the same for Carlotta."

"I hope so," Norman answered.

He could not help wondering to himself how much Carlotta would have done for him.

But when he saw her coming down the stairs, in her going-away dress of pale-coral chiffon with a large straw hat framing her face, he felt he was the luckiest man in the world.

Amid a chorus of farewell kisses and good wishes they got into their car. There was a shower of rice and rose petals, the cheers of their friends, and then they were driven away round the Square.

Norman had planned that they should fly to Paris for the first night of their honeymoon, going on from Paris to Cannes. He could not be away for more than ten days, at the most, and there was every likelihood that he might be recalled.

Things at the works were at their most acute stage. Experiments were taking place and it was imperative that he should be present when the more important decisions had to be made, both with designers and contractors.

He had been working until one o'clock the night before, but now he put all thought of everything from his mind, save the beauty of Carlotta and that she was his wife.

They had a calm passage over the Channel and landed at Le Bourget about tea-time.

Half an hour later they got to the Ritz Hotel, where Norman had booked a suite. Carlotta, entering her rooms, found that they were filled with lilies, the same as those which had decorated the church.

"How lovely!" she said.

The reception clerk left them. Norman went across the room to her.

"Not as lovely as you," he said.

He put out his arms towards her, but at that moment there was a sound outside.

"The luggage," Carlotta said hastily.

He drew away from her.

They had only brought a certain amount with them by air, for Carlotta's newly engaged maid had crossed on the morning boat with the heavier luggage.

While she was unpacking in Carlotta's room, Norman found it difficult to have any private conversation with his wife. He wandered about the sitting-room; then put a call through to his secretary to give him some further instructions.

Before dinner he ordered champagne cocktails, and when Carlotta came from her bedroom, dressed in a floating frock of green chiffon, he thought he had never seen her look more lovely.

She wrapped a cape of dark Russian sables round her before she went downstairs. It had been one of Norman's wedding presents to her. On her wrist she wore another—a bracelet of emeralds and diamonds.

"We will dine at Maxim's," Norman told her. "It is the fashionable place and I expect you would like to show off your new dress."

"I would love to," she answered.

He noted with pride that people looked at Carlotta with interest as she entered the restaurant. It was not surprising for she was outstanding, and, he thought to himself, she had a new dignity which added to her charms.

She smiled at him with a coquettish flash from her eyes, but did not answer.

They talked of many things, of the wedding, of the house and of the parties they must give on their return.

Carlotta was gay; she drank a good deal of champagne

"I love you," he told her suddenly.

"I have never seen you look more wonderful," Norman said, leaning across the table. "You don't look tired, though it has been an exhausting day for both of us."

"I have enjoyed myself," she said. "Fancy, if I had allowed you to have your way and we had been married in some dingy registry office, what we should have missed!"

"You were quite right," he said bravely. "The service was very beautiful."

"Oh, the service," Carlotta said, as if she thought about it for the first time. "Yes, of course, and the reception was fun, wasn't it? Did you hear how funny Magda was being with Sir John Christian? I think your sister Alice was rather shocked."

At one o'clock Norman looked at his watch.

"Oughtn't we to go home?" he asked.

"I would rather like to go on to Montmartre," Carlotta replied.

"Not tonight," Norman said firmly. "I have planned to take you there tomorrow."

She did not protest, but when they got into the taxi to take them to the hotel, he felt that she drew a little away from him, sitting farther into her own corner of the cab than was necessary.

When they reached their sitting-room with its rose-shaded lights shining on the profusion of white lilies, Carlotta stood in the centre of the room.

As she looked towards her husband, following her through the door, he saw that she was pale.

"My darling," he said gently, "you aren't frightened, are you?"

He put out his hand to take hers and realised that she was cold and shivering, although it was a warm, airless night.

"Carlotta," he said, "you know I love you."

"Don't," she said.

She clenched her fists and tried to move away from him. He put out his hands and held her by the shoulders, so that she could not escape.

"What is the matter?" he asked.

"Nothing," she replied, and again she tried to escape him.

Relentlessly he searched her face, refusing to let her go.

"Tell me," he commanded and there was a note of authority in his voice that she had never heard before.

"There is nothing to tell," she said angrily. "Why can't you leave me alone? I won't be bullied."

"I'm not bullying you," Norman said slowly. "Something is wrong, you are trying to avoid me. You don't pretend very well, Carlotta."

"I'm not pretending," she said. "I am tired."

121

"And unhappy?" Norman asked.

"All right then, unhappy," she said with a little flash of anger.

He dropped his hands from her shoulders. She moved quickly away from him, letting the sable cape drop to the floor at his feet. She went towards the window and pulled it wider open. Outside the sky was alight with stars.

"I can't help it," she said at length.

There was a note in her voice as though she was strained beyond breaking point.

"Can't help what?" Norman asked in even tones. "Not loving me? Is that what you mean?"

"I've tried to . . . I've tried to," Carlotta said wildly.

"And now it is too late to do anything about it, you regret the contract?" Norman asked.

"Must you always think in business terms?" Carlotta flashed at him. "Can't you separate your mind from business?"

"I think I understand," he said. "You don't love me, you have never loved me."

"And I have married you for your money!" Carlotta cried hysterically. "Why don't you add that—you are thinking it. I know you are thinking it. Why can't you say so?"

"And you have married me for my money," Norman echoed.

He stood quite still for a moment, then he said:

"For the first time in my life I thought of something except business. I see I was wrong to do so. I have been handed a rotten deal through my own blindness."

He spoke bitterly and his words seemed to sting their way into Carlotta's brain.

She felt a sudden surge of pity, of fear and of apprehension, but because she was overwrought, because she hardly knew what she was saying, she tried to hurt him, to humble him to his knees.

"I am sorry you think that you have got a rotten deal in me," she said, "but at least it is too late now. I am your wife, even though I do love someone else."

"As you say, you are my wife," Norman said gravely.

He walked across the room and opened the door which led to his dressing-room.

"Good night, Carlotta," he said.

He went out, closing the door quietly behind him.

CHAPTER SEVENTEEN

Carlotta awoke with a headache and a sense of depression.

It took her some time to remember where she was and when finally she opened her eyes to see the pale-grey walls and the pink hangings of her bedroom she realised with a feeling of misery that she was alone.

She pressed her hands over her aching eyes, then sat up in bed and tried to collect her thoughts.

'What shall I do? What shall I do?' she asked herself.

She felt, now, that she must have been mad the night before. In her hysterical mood she had said unforgivable things, things which she felt could not be explained away by a light apology or a few smiles.

What was Norman thinking? What had that climax to his wedding day meant to him?

She looked at her clock and was surprised to see that it was nearly half-past ten. Last night she had lain awake for a long time, crying and feeling that sleep would never visit her. When at last it had come she had sunk into the dreamless slumber of exhaustion.

She wished she had the courage to go straight into Norman's room, to tell him how sorry she was. But somehow, she knew that such a course was impossible.

For the first time she thought of him, not as a man in love with her, but as her husband, someone in authority, someone not only to be coquetted with, but to be considered.

'I must think,' she told herself. 'I must approach him in the right way.'

Proudly she told herself that she could erase the past from his mind. After all, the moods and fancies of a bride on her wedding night were understandable.

Norman was not a boy to be devastated by one scene; he was sensible enough to realise that she had been overwrought, that what she had said did not in any way resemble the truth.

She wished, more than anything, that the question of money had not come into their quarrel. She had always sensed that Norman was touchy where money was concerned.

He had not told her in so many words, but she had known, nevertheless, that Evelyn had married him because he was rich. Now she had put herself in the same position.

"Why was I such a fool?" she moaned.

She controlled the tears which from weakness would have sprung to her eyes, and rang the bell beside the bed. When her maid came in she ordered breakfast.

Having had the pillows arranged behind her and having powdered her nose and combed her hair, she decided that she was ready.

"Knock on Sir Norman's door, Elsie," she said, "and ask if he will come in and see me."

She felt the colour rush to her cheeks as she gave the order. She was afraid and embarrassed, but this moment had to be gone through.

Elsie was away for a few minutes. When she returned she had a note in her hand.

"Sir Norman has gone out, my lady," she said, "at least he's not in his room and I found this letter for you on the table in the sitting-room."

Carlotta took it with fingers that shook. Wild thoughts surged through her mind. Had Norman left her? Had he gone back to England?

Was their marriage already at an end? She could hardly control herself enough to open the envelope and read what was written.

There were only a few lines.

Dear Carlotta,
    I have a man to see on business. I shall be downstairs in the bar at one o'clock, ready to give you luncheon.
                                    Yours, Norman.

It was nothing desperate, then, nothing of which she need be afraid. Carlotta could have laughed aloud with relief.

But when she finished her breakfast she opened the note

and reread it. It was cold, she thought, but that of course was understandable.

She remembered Norman's other notes and letters that she had received in the past weeks. They had all started with terms of endearment and always he had signed himself as 'your adoring Norman'.

'I will make it all right,' she told herself confidently.

She lay back on her pillows, planning what she would say and what she would do when they met.

She had an impulse to ring up Magda, to ask her advice, to confide in her as to what had occurred last night. Then, she told herself that a telephone conversation was pointless. It would get her no farther and leave her more uneasy than ever in her own mind.

When Elsie told her that her bath was ready, Carlotta got up quickly. She felt she could not lie in bed any longer. She wanted to move about; she wanted to do something.

It was only midday when she was dressed, wearing one of her new trousseau frocks and a large-brimmed hat.

"I will go downstairs," she said.

As she entered the lounge, she saw a young married couple that she knew coming in from the street.

They greeted her with enthusiasm, for they had always liked Carlotta and found her even more attractive now as the wife of a millionaire. By the name of Drayson, the husband was one of the secretaries at the British Embassy.

His wife, before her marriage, had been one of those artistic, tiresome girls, who take an intense interest in the stage and expound their knowledge of what they call stage technique to anyone who will listen.

Carlotta had often found Baba Drayson a nuisance when she had come into her dressing-room during a busy rehearsal, or at a crowded charity matinée.

Now she was pleased to see her, feeling that in her company some of her depression might be lightened.

"Have you seen the papers, Carlotta, darling?" Baba asked.

Carlotta shook her head.

"There are the most marvellous photographs of you and your husband, really good ones. You are lucky to be so photogenic. Vivian and I looked like gangsters at our wedding."

"I must buy the papers," Carlotta said.

"We'll help you," Baba said excitedly.

They went into the long passage of the Ritz, which

connects the Place Vendome with the rue Cambon. In its centre is the paper stall which has the journals and papers of every country in the world.

Baba had told the truth. Carlotta did look lovely in her photographs, and Norman, smiling as they left the church, looked young and almost handsome.

"I have never seen a happier couple," Vivian said.

Carlotta felt a stab of conscience.

'What would they think,' she asked herself, 'if they knew how we had spent last night'.

"Come and have a drink?" Vivian asked, when they had looked at all the photographs and paid for the papers.

"I am meeting my husband at one o'clock," Carlotta answered.

"There's plenty of time," Baba said, "you have got nearly three-quarters of an hour yet, so you can be our guest in the meantime."

They went through to the bar and sat down at one of the small chromium tables. Vivian ordered champagne cocktails for them all and when they came, Carlotta drank hers gratefully, feeling that it might give her courage.

People came in and out the whole time. Some of them she knew, most of them seemed to be friends of Baba and Vivian.

Carlotta was laughing at the sally of a chance acquaintance when she looked up to see Norman standing in the doorway. Her heart beat quicker and her hands grew cold.

'What shall I do?' she thought rapidly. 'He is before his time!'

Norman looked round the bar casually, then he saw Carlotta. He came across to their table, gravely but with perfect self-composure. It took all her control to say lightly:

"Hullo, darling. I was ready early but luckily I met some old friends of mine."

She introduced Baba and Vivian, who told Norman that they must drink his health.

"We were miserable we couldn't come to your wedding, Sir Norman," Baba said, "but we must wish you every happiness now. We have been looking at the papers." I have never seen two people look happier, so that our wishes aren't really needed."

"But we are very pleased to have them," Norman said gallantly.

Carlotta watched him. She had been afraid, just for a

126

moment, that he might be annoyed to find her with the Draysons.

As it was, he went on talking cheerfully to Baba and even allowed himself to be drawn into a business discussion with Vivian.

It was nearly half-past one before Baba got to her feet.

"We must go," she said. "We are keeping you two poor things from your luncheon. I expect also that you want to be alone."

"Stay and have lunch with us," Norman suggested.

"Oh, but we mustn't," Baba answered. "It would be quite wrong when you are on your honeymoon, wouldn't it, Vivian?"

Vivian hesitated. He was enjoying himself.

"If you are quite sure that you want us," he said.

"But of course we do," Norman said, "don't we, Carlotta?"

It was the first time that he had asked a question of her direct. She flushed as she answered as cordially as she could.

"Of course we do, you must stay."

They all went into the dining room together and after an excellent lunch, Norman suggested that they should drive to the racecourse.

"It would be heaven," Baba said enthusiastically.

She had made it quite clear during the meal that she thought Carlotta was an extremely lucky person to have captured such a charming husband, and Carlotta noted with amusement that she was doing her best to flirt with him.

"Do say you would like it, Carlotta," she pleaded. "I adore racing and Vivian knows lots of the trainers, so we are certain to make money."

"I think it would be very nice," Carlotta answered.

She could not help her voice being a little chilly.

She did not know why, but Baba's gush towards Norman was beginning to irritate her. She had dreaded this meeting with her husband, yet having keyed herself up to it, it was annoying to find herself only an audience, while he and Baba talked and laughed together.

She tried to concentrate on Vivian, but found that he too was more interested in Norman than in herself. She felt she ought to have been glad that things were passing off so easily and lightly. But she was not.

During the whole afternoon she never had a word with Norman alone.

Baba was at his side, asking his advice, introducing him to authorities in the racing world, and keeping up a running flow of conversation the entire time.

Carlotta, who was used to the limelight being focused on herself, tried to find the situation humourous, but by the end of the afternoon she longed to get away from the Draysons and return to the peace and quiet of her own rooms at the hotel.

They drove back into Paris together. As they neared the Ritz, Baba said:

"I suppose there isn't a chance of you coming to the Cafe de Paris tonight? Some friends of ours have got a supper-party and I know they would love to see you. I do wish you would try and come in."

"I think we would love to," Norman said enthusiastically. "That is, on one condition."

"What's that?" Baba asked.

"That you and Vivian will dine with us first," he said.

"But it is too ridiculous!" Baba expostulated, with a pretty expression of shyness and diffidence. "We know what bores we are being, butting in like this. If I was on my honeymoon with you, Sir Norman, I should be furious."

"Carlotta and I have our own ideas on the subject," Norman said, "haven't we, Carlotta?"

Not waiting for her reply, he went on:

"That's settled, then. You and Vivian go home and change, come straight up to our suite when you are ready and we'll have cocktails. We will dine at Larue and have a really good meal before we face the crowds of the Cafe de Paris."

"How too, too lovely," Baba said, clapping her hands together affectedly. "You really are a marvellous person, Sir Norman. Carlotta, I think you are the luckiest girl in the world!"

Carlotta smiled with an effort. She was angry, but afraid to show it. For perhaps the first time since she had known him, she wanted to be with Norman alone.

'I will talk to him before dinner,' she told herself, and felt again that tremor of fear and excitement.

But this time she welcomed it, for once she knew Norman's attitude towards her, that miserable sense of anticipation which had been haunting her ever since she woke would be annihilated.

When they reached their suite, her plans were circumvented. Norman, having opened the door into the sitting-room, said:

"I have got some important telephone calls to do, Carlotta. I know you will excuse me until dinner-time. Let's meet here at a quarter to nine."

Carlotta was too surprised to speak. As he reached the door of his room, she stopped him.

"Norman," she said, "I want to talk to you."

He paused, the door open, his hand on the handle.

"I am sorry," he answered firmly, "but this is business. I feel sure you will understand."

He left her and she stood alone in the flower-filled room, shaken with anger. She rushed into her own room and slammed the door, but it did not relieve her feelings.

She lay down on her bed and asked her maid to bring her an aspirin and a handkerchief soaked in eau de Cologne, as she had a headache. But she could not rest.

When Elsie had gone, she got up and walked about the room. Suddenly an idea came to her.

She had taken off her dress to lie down and was wrapped in a rest gown of soft chiffon and lace. Tinted to deep coral it made her look vividly lovely and very appealing.

She powdered her nose again, sprayed some scent over her hair and neck. Trembling a little at what she was about to do, she walked towards the door of Norman's room and knocked . . .

There was no answer. She waited a few moments, then knocked again. Still there was no reply.

She hesitated, then, flinging back her head with a gesture of defiance, turned the handle of the door.

It was locked.

CHAPTER EIGHTEEN

The golden sunshine was glittering on the deep azure blue of the Mediterranean; far out to sea the faint haze over the horizon made it shimmer where the sky met the sea.

On the hills behind Cannes, the trees were verdant and the gardens ablaze with the summer flowers.

Carlotta lay on her balcony alone. A large green-and-white umbrella protected her head from the sun, but her neck and arms were bare and her dress was cut low at the back.

In the past few days she had begun to brown slowly, her skin taking on a faintly golden hue as though it had become impregnated with the radiant sunshine which suffused everything.

Carlotta did not look happy. Her eyes were tired and dark-rimmed, her mouth drooped at the corners.

It was Norman who had suggested that she should rest after luncheon each day and she had agreed.

She had learnt to agree to everything that he wanted, while dreading the two long hours which she must spend alone in her own bedroom or on the balcony.

Carlotta had only been married for a week, but she had already learnt that the man who was her husband was not in the least the person she had imagined him to be.

Since their first night in Paris he had been a complete stranger to her. The three days and nights that they had spent there were to Carlotta like a nightmare.

Norman had surrounded himself with friends, and she had been unable to approach him, unable to have a conversation with him alone. He had given parties, and she had been obliged to fulfil the role of hostess.

They had raced, they had been to theatres, they had visited every fashionable restaurant, they had even done a certain amount of sightseeing, but always they had been accompanied by a crowd of laughing, chattering people.

130

Carlotta was not certain where they had all come from or how they had been collected. Only one thing was common to them all—their willingness to spend Norman's money for him.

Carlotta was weary, mentally and physically, when she stepped from the Blue Train which brought them to Cannes. In the flaming sunshine she had felt that the beauty of everything must in some way prove a good augury for her future happiness.

'I can't go on like this,' she told herself. 'I can't, I can't.'

At last she had the opportunity of saying so to Norman.

The morning had been spent unpacking, but after luncheon was over they had gone upstairs to their suite. They had found no servants there. For the first time for days they had a moment alone.

"You would like to rest, I expect," Norman said courteously.

He was unexceptionally polite to Carlotta, showing her attention which she loathed, because she felt they were false and assumed.

"Norman," she said, "I want to talk to you. Please listen to me."

"But of course," he answered, "what is it you want to say?"

"I have been trying to speak to you for days," she said nervously, "but we have been so surrounded with friends, at least you have, that I haven't had an opportunity."

"I am sorry," he said, "I thought you were enjoying the entertainments I arranged for you. They cost a lot of money."

Carlotta flushed.

"Norman," she said, "you are being horrid to me."

"Horrid!" he said. "I am afraid I don't understand. I have been doing everything in my power to make our honeymoon amusing."

"Oh, be honest," Carlotta said impatiently. "You are doing nothing of the sort. You are filling up our time with ridiculous, stupid people, whom neither of us care anything about."

"In that case," Norman said, "I am sorry. I thought that the Draysons were your friends and that you liked them."

"It isn't that," Carlotta said wearily. "It is us, Norman, I am sorry about the other night . . . terribly sorry."

"My dear child," Norman replied. "Please don't worry about a little thing like that."

"Norman, you aren't being real, you aren't being genuine with me," Carlotta said desperately. "Don't you understand? I was mad, overwrought, hysterical, and I said a lot of things that I didn't mean. Must you go on punishing me?"

Norman looked at her. It seemed to her that he had eyes made of steel.

"There is nothing to apologise for," he said. "I assure you. I like the truth—I have always liked it."

"But it wasn't the truth," Carlotta said. "I swear to you, Norman, that what I said was not true."

Norman walked across the room towards her. He did not touch her, but he stood very close, looking down into her face.

"Look at me!" he commanded.

She was trembling, but she forced herself to raise her face to his, to look him in the eyes, even while her mouth quivered and she clenched her hands together convulsively.

"Will you swear to me on the Bible, on all that you hold sacred," Norman said, "that you love me for myself?"

Carlotta was paralysed; she could not speak; her tongue seemed to cleave to the roof of her mouth; her lips were dry. She could only stare at him and then drop her eyes beneath his.

He gave a short laugh which held no humour, only a bitterness that was beyond words. Then he left her alone.

For some minutes she stood still, then she dropped to the sofa sobbing as though her heart would break.

When they met again Norman was exactly as he had been before. He talked to her, but only as he would talk to a casual acquaintance to whom he was being particularly polite.

They did things together, but Carlotta felt as though she ate, walked and danced with an automaton. She was up against a barrier which she could not bridge. She had never in the whole of her life encountered anything so difficult, so incomprehensible, as the distance which yawned between Norman and herself.

She did not know what to do. She was lost, a child in a forest of fears and terrors which were all the greater because they were hidden behind the conventionalities of politeness.

'I can't bear it . . . I can't, she told herself a thousand times.

She tried to flirt with Norman; she tried to entice him

132

into some uncontrolled expression of himself; she tried being defiant, aloof and exasperating. He remained exactly the same, a creature of stone.

She could make no impression upon him.

The second day that they were at Cannes he came into her room before dinner with a pink leather box in his hand. Elsie was dressing her and both she and Carlotta looked up in surprise as Norman entered.

It was the first time he had come to her bedroom and Carlotta's heart gave a leap of excitement. Did this mean the beginning of a new era?

She made a gesture towards Elsie, but Norman saw it.

"Don't go, Elsie," he said genially. "I have brought her ladyship a present and I expect you would like to see it too."

"A present!" Carlotta said in surprise.

"All brides receive presents on their honeymoon," Norman said. "Didn't you know that?"

"No, I didn't know," Carlotta said weakly.

"Open it and see if you approve," he suggested.

He held the pink box out to her. She took it from him.

Inside was a huge brooch of emeralds and diamonds. It was a magnificent though flamboyant piece of jewellery, which could be worn either in one piece or as two clips.

At any other time Carlotta would have gone into ecstasies of excitement at receiving such a present. Now, for some inexplicable reason, she wanted to cry.

"My lady, it is magnificent," Elsie exclaimed over her shoulder.

"Do you like it, Carlotta?" Norman said.

"It is very . . . beautiful," she answered, but there was a sob in her voice.

"Well, wear it then tonight," he said: "I expect you have a dress that will match it. If not, we shall have to see about getting you one."

He left the room. Carlotta looked at the glittering brooch.

"Sir Norman is so kind," Elsie said. "It is a lovely present, my lady. It will look wonderful on your white dress."

Carlotta got to her feet abruptly.

"Yes, bring me my white dress," she said. "I have an idea."

"An idea?" Elsie said.

"Did I say that?" Carlotta asked. "I was thinking aloud.

Bring me my white dress, Elsie, and I will wear green sandals with it."

She dressed, taking a long time over the process, so that she knew Norman would be waiting for her in the sitting-room.

When she was ready she clipped her emerald-and-diamond bracelet on her wrist, put her engagement ring on her finger, and, picking up the new brooch in her hand went into the sitting-room.

Norman, as she expected, was ready before her. He was standing looking out of the window. Night had fallen quickly. The sea, moving restlessly, was but a deeper purple echo of the sky above it. Stars hovered like glittering jewels.

Everything was very still and there was the sweet-scented fragrance of a Mediterranean night coming through the open windows.

Carlotta stood just inside the sitting-room, looking at Norman's square shoulders. She thought how nice he looked in his evening clothes and, for the first time, there came to her the idea that he was desirable as a lover . . .

She had only thought about Hector in that way, never any other man. Now she told herself that some women would be glad to be loved by Norman and even she, who loved someone else, felt herself almost attracted to him.

'I will make him love me again,' she told herself. 'I will make him confess it. It is there. I believe it is there. He is only hiding it, only trying to punish me because he is hurt by what I said.'

Determinedly she advanced to the centre of the room.

"Norman," she said, very gently.

He turned round abruptly as she said his name—she knew that his thoughts had been far away. 'With his business,' she guessed jealously.

"Are you ready?" he said.

"Quite ready," she answered, "except for my brooch."

She held it out towards him.

"What is wrong?" he asked.

"Nothing's wrong," Carlotta said with a smile, "but it is usual on such occasions to pin the present on the bride."

She looked at him, hoping that some expression would change his courteous severity, to which she had grown so used.

"Is that the custom?" he said. "I had no idea. How remiss of me."

134

He came towards her, unclipping the pin of the brooch from its catch.

"Where do you want to wear it?" he asked.

She pointed to the V of her dress, cut low between her breasts.

'Surely this will move something within him,' she told herself, but his hand did not tremble, and outwardly he remained unmoved.

It was Carlotta who quivered as she felt his fingers fumbling with the brooch, catching it with difficulty into the thin chiffon of her gown.

His head was bent, it was within a few inches of hers; she knew that the seductive scent she was using must be in his nostrils. He must be conscious of her nearness, and of the quickening beat of her heart.

"Is that right?" he asked, and stood back to view his handiwork with the air of a man who had completed a difficult task.

"Is it straight?" Carlotta asked, looking at him.

She knew that she was desirable, knew that her air of humble attention would force any other man to his knees, would excite the senses of anyone who was not made of iron.

"Quite straight," Norman answered. "I really think it looks very nice. It cost a lot of money."

Carlotta choked.

"Must you always mention the price of things?" she asked.

"But that is what interests you, surely?" he asked. "You want full value, my dear Carlotta, you have told me so, and I have promised myself that you shall have it.

"By the way," he added, "we shall be returning to London in two days' time. I have to get back, you know, because of my work. I have instructed my bank to pay an allowance to you quarterly and it is deposited in your name.

"You will find a statement and a cheque book awaiting you at Belgrave Square. If, however, you require any money in the meantime, you have only to ask me."

"I don't want your money," Carlotta said in an angry voice.

"It is nice of you to say that," Norman answered, "but I think you will find it very useful and, of course, as my wife, you will have a large number of expenses that have never occurred previously."

"Am I your wife?" Carlotta asked bitterly. "It is a strange sort of honeymoon, isn't it?"

"My dear Lady Melton," Norman said with a low bow, "you must be tired. Let me take you down to dinner. You will feel better after food and a bottle of champagne. I have ordered one and it is already on the ice."

"Can't you be human for one moment?" Carlotta asked.

"Let's go down to dinner," he replied.

She wanted to cry out at him. Throw the presents he had given her in his face, shut herself in her own room and refuse to come out, but she knew it would do no good. On the morrow they would be in exactly the same position as before.

She hesitated, and while she did so, Norman went to her bedroom door.

"Her ladyship's wrap, Elsie," he called. "We shall be going to the Casino after dinner."

Elsie came in, carrying a cape of white foxes.

"Will you have this, my lady?" she asked, "or would you prefer the green velvet?"

"The white foxes," Norman answered for her. "The emeralds as the only touch of colour are quite perfect. I see that I shall have to give you earrings as my next present, Carlotta, perhaps on the anniversary of our wedding day. That would be a delightful way of celebrating a year's happiness, wouldn't it?"

Carlotta pulled the foxes round her shoulders with a weary gesture.

"I can't see so far ahead," she said. "A year is a very long time."

"It will pass very quickly," he promised her, and opened the door.

"Good night, Elsie," he said.

"Good night, Sir Norman," Elsie answered, "and good night, my lady. I hope you will have a happy evening."

"I hope so too," Carlotta said, looking at Norman.

"Undoubtedly we will," he replied.

But he spoke in the voice that she hated and which already she feared more than she had ever feared anything else in her life.

CHAPTER NINETEEN

Alice bustled from room to room at 'The Paddocks', re-arranging the flowers that she had already done earlier that morning, flicking imaginary specks of dust from the tables, and shaking the curtains so that they fell into neater and more dignified folds.

She was determined that everything should be in spick-and-span order for Norman and his bride.

When Carlotta arrived, dressed in pale-grey with furs to match, a huge buttonhole of crimson carnations pinned to her lapel, Alice knew that Norman was changed.

Something had upset him; something had driven away the expression of happiness which during the month before his wedding had been frequently in his eyes.

She wondered what was the matter. Only when there had been a strike at the works, or a breakdown involving loss of life, had she known him to look so grim, so uncompromisingly severe.

She went forward to kiss Carlotta before she lifted her face to receive her brother's dutiful caress.

"Have you had a good journey?" she asked.

"Very," he said abruptly.

Alice, knowing his moods, understood that he wanted to remain unquestioned, to go into the house and to escape the greetings and congratulations which both she and the staff were ready to offer him.

Finally, after Carlotta had shaken hands with the upper servants, they found themselves alone in the morning-room. Alice somewhat nervously asked Carlotta if she would like to see the house.

"I would like to see my bedroom most of all," Carlotta answered. "I am tired and dusty. I feel as if I have been travelling for weeks."

"Well, do come up," Alice replied. "I have got ready the big south room for you. I thought you would like it best, but, of course, things can easily be changed round if you see another that you like better."

"Oh, any room will do for the moment," Carlotta said indifferently.

She did not look at her husband, and, indeed, made no attempt to speak to him, so that Alice felt there must be some disagreement between them, one which had been interrupted by their arrival, and had thus reached no climax.

'Oh dear, oh dear,' she thought. 'I do hope that Norman is going to be happy.'

She led Carlotta upstairs, pointing out, as she did so, the doors of the library and the morning-room.

"This is the south room," she said as they reached the first landing.

She opened the door into a big bow-windowed room, into which the sunlight was streaming. The furniture was old-fashioned, but seemed perfectly in harmony with the great four-poster bed with its tasselled hangings and the yellow brocade curtains which had faded with age until they were like mellow sunlight.

Carlotta walked across to the dressing-table, and pulling her small grey hat from her head, put it down with a sense of relief.

"I am tired," she said.

"Would you like something to eat or drink?" Alice asked. "Norman told me that you would have luncheon on the way up, otherwise something would have been prepared for you."

"No, I don't need anything," Carlotta answered. "I didn't sleep well last night. I hate a sleeper and we had rather a rough crossing. Norman wanted to fly. I wish now I had agreed, but I am not my best in the air."

"I have never been up," Alice said timidly. "I know it sounds very cowardly, but I really can't brave it."

"That's not the right remark for Norman's sister, is it?" Carlotta said jokingly.

"Don't mention it to him, please," Alice begged. "I don't think he has ever realised that I have never left the ground. If he once got it into his head I should have to go. I really think I should die of fear."

"I won't breathe a word, I promise you," Carlotta said, then added curiously: "Are you afraid of Norman?"

Alice flushed, a difficult, ugly flush of old age, which suffused her pale cheeks a vivid scarlet.

"No, of course not!" she said hurriedly. "He is very kind to me always, as I am sure he is to you."

"Oh, very kind," Carlotta said.

There was such bitterness in her tone that Alice could not fail to notice it.

"My dear," she said impulsively, then checked herself. It was no business of hers to interfere in the intimate lives of her brother and of this singularly beautiful girl he had married.

Carlotta, however, turned round to look at her.

"What were you going to say?" she asked.

"Nothing," Alice said hurriedly, "nothing at all."

Then under Carlotta's quizzical, unbelieving eyes, she added:

"Your voice sounded unhappy. Of course, it was my mistake, but I just thought that for a moment."

"You weren't mistaken," Carlotta said in a quiet voice.

Alice started.

"Oh dear," she said, "you mean you aren't happy? How terrible. What can I do? How can I help you?"

"No one can help me," Carlotta said. "It is entirely my own fault, but there it is. A nice homecoming for a bride, isn't it?"

"What can I do?" Alice asked miserably. "I must help you, you must let me."

"I am a fool to have said anything about it," Carlotta said. "I must manage my own troubles. I am old enough."

She shrugged her shoulders.

"Come and show me the house," she said. "Norman tells me you are leaving 'The Paddocks'. Is that true?"

"Quite true," Alice answered. The tone of her voice changed—it became one of excited anticipation.

"Must you leave us?" Carlotta said carelessly. "I would love you to stay, you know."

"Oh!" Alice's exclamation was one of drawn-out horror and despondency.

"But you don't want to stay!" Carlotta said. "Then of course you must go. I thought perhaps you minded giving up this house to me."

"I don't mind at all," Alice said hastily. "You see, Norman has bought a little house for me—one we had before. It is only very small, but I love it. I am happy there."

She hesitated. Then made the one heroic gesture of her life.

"But if you want me to stay," she said slowly, "if you would really like me to, Carlotta, of course I will."

Carlotta shook her head.

"I wouldn't keep you from your little house for anything in the world," she said.

"Are you quite sure?" Alice said doubtfully.

"Quite sure," Carlotta answered.

They walked round the house together, Carlotta taking very little interest in the number of bedrooms, dressing-rooms and bathrooms, most of which were shuttered and under dust sheets.

When they reached the ground floor, she had of her new home only an impression of emptiness. The drawing room was formal and desolate, lacking the finishing touches which only a woman can give if she loves a house and is proud of it.

The library was Norman's own particular place for work and for relaxation. There was something typical of him in the atmosphere of severity, and in the book-lined walls.

The desk was piled high with letters and documents which had been waiting his return. He was reading a newspaper when they entered, and got to his feet slowly, without a word of greeting.

"I am showing Carlotta the house," Alice said nervously.

Carlotta noticed that she was afraid of her brother, that her attitude towards him was one of nervous deference, as though she expected him to contradict every word she said.

"Does she like it?" Norman said.

Carlotta was annoyed at his tone and the way he had not addressed her direct. A faint smile curled her lips.

"There is plenty of room for nurseries, isn't there, Norman?" she said.

Alice gave a little choke of surprise, but Norman looked directly at Carlotta.

She saw an angry light blaze forth into his eyes and knew by the tightening of his mouth that he was furious with her.

She laughed. Then linking her arm through Alice's she drew her towards the door.

"There's time for that, though," she said, over her shoulder. "Good-bye, Norman, we won't disturb you any longer."

She was pleased with herself for having hurt him, for having for once had the advantage over him in a passage of wits. But she did not know that when the door of the library shut behind her Norman sank down in his chair, and buried his face in his hands.

He sat for a long time without moving. Finally, with a deep sigh which seemed to come from the depths of his heart, he got up and walked towards the desk. He sat looking at the pile of letters and papers.

Then he braced himself as though he thrust from him some intolerable burden, and settled down to work.

It was nearly an hour later and he was still hard at work when the telephone rang beside him. He picked up the receiver and listened to a voice at the other end for several minutes in silence.

Then he said curtly:

"I will come down right away."

He rang the bell for the butler and ordered his car to be brought round at once.

"As quickly as possible," he commanded. "It is urgent."

"Very good, Sir Norman," the butler answered. "Won't you have a cup of tea before you go? It is ready in the morning-room."

"Is her ladyship there?" Norman questioned.

"I think so, Sir Norman."

Norman walked to the door of the morning-room and opened it. He saw, sitting by the window, Carlotta and Alice.

"I am going down to the works," he said, speaking to both of them. "There has been an accident in the workshops. I don't know when I shall be back."

"An accident" Alice said. "I hope no one has been really hurt."

Norman did not answer her. He had already closed the door behind him, hurried across the hall and was waiting impatiently on the doorstep when his car arrived.

"What do you think has happened?" Carlotta said.

"I don't know," Alice said. "Sometimes the accident is quite a slight one, but once, nearly six years ago, one of the men was killed and Norman was most terribly upset. It was no one's fault—he slipped and fell into the machinery—but, of course, there were inquests and inquiries—all very upsetting."

"Do you ever go down to the works yourself?" Carlotta asked.

Alice shook her head.

"I have only been round them twice," she answered. "Once when Norman first took them over, and again when he was made a baronet. They had a sort of party there and I was told to escort some visitors on a tour of inspection."

"I'd like to go there," Carlotta said. "I want to see what it is that takes up at least three-quarters of Norman's thoughts."

"I think they took up the whole until you came along," Alice said shyly.

"I don't think I have made much difference," Carlotta answered bitterly. "I expect you will find that he will be just as efficient and just as dedicated to big business as he was in the past."

"I hope not," Alice said. "Norman has always been such a very lonely person. At times he has been desperately unhappy."

"Has he?" Carlotta said in surprise.

It sounded strange to her to hear Norman being pitied by this funny, old-fashioned sister of his.

"He was very unhappy in his first marriage," Alice said. "I knew that. I used to see him a great deal, for Evelyn never came to Melchester. She only liked living in London. When Norman would have to stay up for the night, he would stay with me and he invariably came home for lunch, unless the pressure of work was too much for him."

"Why was he so unhappy?" Carlotta asked.

"She was very proud," Alice said. "And she was cruel to him."

"Cruel!" Carlotta echoed.

"Perhaps that is not the right word," Alice said. "It is rather difficult to explain what I mean, but she always spoke as though she despised him. She despised me too, of course I expected that. After all, I am nobody, and she was a lady, very well-born, with generations behind her."

"How ridiculous!" Carlotta said. "I can hardly believe it. Don't you think that perhaps she meant to be nice and was just bad at expressing her feelings?"

"I don't think she had any feelings," Alice said. "She was like a statue, beautiful, still, and cold. I almost expected her to be made of marble."

"Poor Norman," Carlotta said, and for the moment she really meant it.

"Once," Alice went on, "Norman confessed to me that he had made a mistake. You must never tell him that I told you because he would hate me for betraying his confidence. He is pathetic at times. I can't help feeling that you and he will be happy together. You were just tired when you arrived and perhaps you had a little disagreement. Lovers often do have them, don't they?"

"Very often," Carlotta said dryly.

"You see, you are so pretty and so young, so different from everything that Evelyn was," Alice said. "What Norman wants is mothering, being made a fuss of, of having someone glad to see him when he comes home in the evenings from work, of belonging to someone.

"It is funny I should be telling you this, but I have often thought about it to myself. I am such a silly person where Norman is concerned. I find it very difficult to talk to him.

"He talks to me, but I can't say the right things. I'm sure you will be able to manage him, be able to give him all the things he has always wanted."

"What has he wanted?" Carlotta said. "Surely he has got everything in the world!"

"Everything in the world!" Alice said in surprise; "surely you don't think he has got that because he has got money? He is alone—don't you see? He has no friends in the class to which he belongs and he has made none in the class to which he has risen.

"I am the same too, but it doesn't matter for me, and anyway, things will be so much better now I can go back to my little house. There are a few neighbours with whom I can occasionally take a cup of tea, but Norman's different.

"He is so ambitious, Melchester people were never good enough for him once he began to rise, and the London people—people like Evelyn—didn't really want him, they only wanted his money.

"Oh, I know I ought not to say all this, but I have seen it, known it for so many years, and bottled it up inside myself. He has come back to me sometimes from one of those grand parties in London and I have known that he has not enjoyed himself. People have either snubbed him or gushed at him so insincerely that he has seen through them.

"He has got nothing except money out of all his years of hard work, and now he has got it, he doesn't know what to do with it."

"I have never thought of him like that," Carlotta said slowly.

"But now everything can be changed," Alice went on earnestly. "You can help him; you can make him feel he isn't alone, a stranger among all those grand stuck-up people. You are so pretty they will be glad to welcome you anyway, whether you have money or not."

"An unknown actress?" Carlotta asked with a smile.

"That has got nothing to do with it," Alice said. "You have got the one thing that matters, as far as I can see, in society—assurance, perhaps I should say confidence in yourself. You show it in the way you walk, the way you shake hands and smile. But Norman hasn't got it—not quite. You will teach him, won't you, Carlotta?"

Looking into Alice's eyes, into her earnest face, strained with the task of putting into words her intimate thoughts, Carlotta answered quickly and with sincerity:

"I will try, I promise you."

CHAPTER TWENTY

Norman paced up and down the small waiting room of the hospital. Without thinking he took a cigarette out of his case.

When he was about to light it, he remembered that it was better not to smoke in such surroundings, and replaced it. He looked at his watch. He had been waiting for nearly twenty minutes.

The loud tick of the clock on the mantelpiece was the only sound to be heard, except for the steady beat of his own feet. His brain asked the same question over and over again, could such an accident have been prevented?

They had spent large sums only the year before in safety devices.

Norman had personally thought that they were foolproof, and yet there had been three minor mishaps in the last five months and now a major accident.

He started as the door opened and the surgeon came in.

"I am sorry, Melton," he said. "I could do nothing."

"The man is dead?" Norman questioned.

"He died on the operating table. There was nothing we could have done, anyway. The skull was completely crushed."

They spoke together for a few moments, then Norman went downstairs to where his car was waiting. As he reached it another car came hurrying into the courtyard and his secretary got out.

"Have you the particulars?"

His secretary handed him a sheaf of papers.

"Shall I go down to his home, Sir Norman?" he asked. Norman shook his head.

"I will go myself. Walker was one of our best men."

"He was indeed, Sir Norman. As you will see he has been with us nearly ten years. Is there a chance of saving him?"

"None," Norman answered shortly. "He died on the operating table."

"I am sorry," the secretary said.

Norman got into his own car and gave an address; the chauffeur drove off.

After half a mile of the main roadway they turned into the squalid dirty slums of Melchester. There had been local agitation about them for some time; the housing problem was growing acute. Very little, as yet, had been done.

Norman noted the narrow pavements on which the children were playing, the cracked panes of glass in many of the windows, the crooked, badly fitting doors to the houses, and the small, grimy bricks, all of which needed repointing.

He felt that he had neglected many opportunities in the past when he might have demanded the abolition of these houses.

He knew quite well that there had been talk of building a housing estate some way out from the town. He had heard it proposed many times.

He had read about it in the local papers, but always he had been too busy with his own factory, too concerned about his own works, to pay much attention to the homes of his workmen.

He saw now that he had been at fault. He had been scrupulously fair about their wages.

He had worked them shorter hours than most other employers in the country, but he had not worried about the homes from which they came, or concerned himself with their standard of living once they had left his own boundaries.

He remembered now, more vividly than he had for years, the insides of these airless and often insanitary houses; he remembered the black beetles, the bugs that would come out at night, the mice and rats, which it was impossible to exterminate.

The impulse came to him to help the people from which he had sprung. He would fight their battles. He would be their champion.

'I have been lucky,' he told himself, 'lucky all my life and because of it I must make things brighter for these people. Fortune doesn't smile on them. I can do it and I will do it.'

The car drew up and he found himself facing a row of

houses, all identical, all indistinguishable in their squalid sordidness from each other.

"This is the place, sir," his chauffeur said, opening the door.

Norman walked up the three steps which led directly from the pavement to the door, and knocked on it with his knuckles.

Almost immediately it was opened and a voice said:

"Thank goodness you have come, but I am afraid you will be too late."

He found himself looking at a small, plump, little woman.

"I am sorry," she added before he could speak, "I thought you were the doctor."

He saw by her uniform that she was the district nurse.

"Is anything the matter?"

"Everything," she said briefly. "Mrs. Walker's just had a severe miscarriage. I have sent a boy for the doctor, but I am afraid he is out."

"Can my chauffeur do anything?" Norman asked.

"Well, if Dr. Matthews is at his surgery, he would have come by now," Nurse said, "and if he's out on his rounds, goodness knows where we will find him."

"What about another doctor?" Norman suggested.

"There's Dr. Martin in Cheapside Road," she replied, "if you could get him."

Norman turned back towards the car and gave the necessary instructions.

"As quick as you can," he said, "it is a matter of life and death."

He turned back to find that the nurse had already disappeared. He could hear footsteps moving above, overhead. He went into the room and prepared to wait.

It was a very small, somewhat congested kitchen, but it was scrupulously clean. The table and the floor had obviously been freshly scrubbed and there were sheets of fresh newspaper arranged around the stove to prevent anything from spilling on to the clean flags.

He was about to sit down in an arm-chair, when there was a movement from behind it and out scrambled a small boy.

"Hullo," Norman said, "I didn't know that you were there."

"I'm playing twains," the small boy said with dignity but with difficulty over his r's, "and I've gone into a tunnel."

147

Norman laughed and sat down in the chair. The child got to his feet. He could not have been more than six years old.

He was a particularly nice-looking little boy, with a clean jumper and dark-blue shorts, which had been patched in several places.

"My Mummy's ill," he said, "and I've got to be vewy quiet."

"That's a good boy," Norman said.

"When my Daddy comes home," the child went on, "he will take me for a wide on his bicycle. He pwomised me."

Norman felt his heart contract with pity. From what the nurse had said, the woman upstairs was in danger of her life.

"Who else lives here?" he asked, "besides your Daddy and Mummy."

"Only me," the boy answered.

"And what is your name?" Norman said.

"Billy," was the reply. "My weal name is William, but eve'yone calls me Billy."

"Well, Billy," Norman said, "haven't you got an aunty or a grandmother who comes to see you sometimes?"

Billy shook his head.

"My Gwandma's in heaven," he said, "my Mummy said so."

"And what about an aunty or uncle?" Norman asked.

"No aunties," Billy said stubbornly.

He spoke as though he were not quite certain what they were.

Norman was nonplussed and was wondering what to ask next when there was the sound of a car driving up outside.

A second later the door flew open, and a short man with grey hair and a grey moustache came hurrying into the room. He carried the inevitable doctor's bag in his hands and Norman recognised him as Dr. Matthews.

The doctor was obviously surprised to see Norman.

"Good heavens, Melton," he said. "It is you, isn't it?"

"Yes," Norman answered, "but don't waste time talking to me. There's trouble upstairs. Nurse is waiting for you."

The doctor needed no further urging, but hurried up the rickety staircase to the room above.

"Do you think my Mummy will soon be well?" Billy asked uneasily. "I want my tea."

"Haven't you had it?" Norman asked.

The small boy shook his head.

"The milk's come," he said, pointing to a jug on the dresser, "but nu'se said not to touch."

Norman got up, took down the milk, and poured some into a cup.

"I will give it to you," he said cheerily, "and we will explain to Nurse afterwards. What about some bread and butter? Do you know where the bread is kept?"

Under Billy's directions Norman found half a loaf of bread and a small pat of margarine in a cupboard. He cut some for the small boy who settled himself at the table with an air of contentment.

"You have some too," he invited hospitably.

Norman shook his head.

"I'm not hungry," he said.

"I'm always hungwy," Billy announced. "Daddy says I eat too much."

Norman glanced at his watch and wondered how long it would be before the doctor could give him news of the child's mother.

As he put his watch away there was the sound of footsteps on the staircase and Dr. Matthews came into the room, a solemn expression on his face. Without asking, Norman knew that Billy's mother was dead.

"Come outside, Matthews," he said, "I want to speak to you a moment."

The doctor did as he was asked, patting Billy on the head as he passed and saying kindly:

"Enjoying your tea, old man?"

"He got it," Billy said, pointing a finger at Norman.

Doctor Matthews looked at Norman.

"You haven't told me yet why you are here," he said.

The two men went down the steps, shutting the door behind them. They walked up the street.

"Walker had an accident this afternoon," Norman said. "He died in hospital."

"Good God!" Doctor Matthews ejaculated.

"And his wife?" Norman asked.

"Dead," Matthews replied. "A hemorrhage. If the nurse could have got me in time I might have been able to do something but I doubt it."

Norman was silent.

"What will happen to the child?" he asked.

Dr. Matthews shrugged his shoulders.

"He will have to go to a home, I suppose," he said. "He

has no relations that I know of. We can inquire, of course, but Walker was not a Melchester man originally. He came from Birmingham about fifteen years ago. His wife is a local girl; both her parents are dead. I knew them well and attended them; she was an only child."

"I am worried about that child," Norman said.

"Poor little devil," the doctor replied. "He's a nice boy, too, fond of his parents and they adored him. His mother was thrilled at the idea of having another child. She came to see me soon after it was started. She was a frail-looking woman, but I thought she would be all right. It is generally the robust-looking ones that let one down."

They walked back the way they had come and stopped at the door of the house.

"Nurse will see to everything," the doctor said. "I have got another patient the other side of the town. I shall have to be getting off to her. I think it is twins this time."

"What are you going to do about the boy?" Norman asked.

"By jove! I must do something," the doctor said. "I had better ask Nurse if she knows anyone who can see to him tonight. Then I will run out to the orphanage in the morning and have a word with the superintendent."

"I will take him for tonight," Norman said impetuously.

"You!" the doctor ejaculated.

Forgetting his manners he stared at Norman in bewilderment.

"Yes, I will take him," Norman repeated.

"But where?" the doctor said. "You mean to 'The Paddocks'. But surely you have just returned from your honeymoon. What will your wife say?"

"There's plenty of room at 'The Paddocks'," Norman said.

"I must say it is uncommon good of you, Melton. I will speak to the superintendent in the morning and tell him where the child is."

"Thank you," Norman answered.

"We will tell Nurse," the doctor said, opening the door of the house. "The child must have some things to take with him."

Billy had finished his tea and had arranged his cup and several plates in a pyramid, standing one on top of the other.

"Steady, Billy," the doctor said as he came in. "You will be smashing something that way."

"I am building a big house," Billy answered, "and there are lions inside it."

Norman walked across to the table.

"Listen, Billy," he said. "Would you like to come with me and see a very big house? There aren't any lions, I am afraid, but the house is there; all right?"

"How should we go there?" Billy asked practically.

"In my car," Norman answered.

"In that car outside?" Billy asked wide-eyed.

"Yes, in that one," Norman answered.

"I'll go," Billy said enthusiastically. "Can my Mummy come too?"

"I am afraid not," Norman said. "Mummy's very ill and I think she would like you to come and stay with me tonight at my house. She would want you to be a good boy."

"I'll be a vewy good boy," Billy said, "if I go in the big car. I'll tell my Mummy."

He turned towards the stairs, but Norman stopped him.

"Wait a minute," he said, a hand on the child's shoulder. "You mustn't go up and disturb your mother."

Nurse came downstairs a few moments later with the doctor. She carried a pathetically small brown paper parcel in which were all Billy's worldly possessions. Over her arm was a grey coat, tattered and torn with only one button to fasten it.

She helped Billy into it and gave him the parcel.

"There's a tooth-brush there," she said, "and a shirt to wear in bed tonight. Don't forget to use the tooth-brush, Billy."

She turned to Norman.

"I am sorry, Sir Norman," she said, "that I didn't recognise you when you came, but I was so upset at what was happening—you understand?"

"Of course I understand," Norman answered. "I will look after Billy and the doctor will see to him tomorrow."

"It is a relief to me," Nurse answered.

"Come along," Norman said to the child.

Billy hung back.

"Can I just call goodbye to my Mummy?" he asked, "that won't wowwy her, will it?"

"No, that won't disturb her," she said, "but you mustn't expect her to answer. She is very ill, you know."

Billy cupped his mouth with both his small hands.

"Good-bye Mummy," he shouted. "I'll be back tomow-ow. I am going in a big car. I'll be a very good boy."

He took his hands away from his mouth.

"Do you think she heard me?" he asked anxiously.

"I am sure she did," the nurse answered.

Norman put his hand towards Billy. He did not look at Dr. Matthews. In silence they went down the steps of the house and entered the car.

Billy got in beside Norman. He was pale with excitement and his eyes were wide with wonder.

"It is a vewy big car," he said, in awed tones.

"It is one of the ones I make," Norman explained as they started off.

"My Daddy makes cars too," Billy answered. "Do you work with my Daddy?"

"Yes," Norman replied.

"Did you and Daddy make this car?" Billy asked.

"Yes, we did."

"When I am gwown up I will make cars too," Billy said.

"I hope you will," Norman answered.

"Melton cars are better than any other cars," Billy said. "My Daddy says so."

Norman laughed.

"Do you know what my name is?" he asked.

"You didn't tell me," Billy replied.

"My name is Melton," Norman announced.

Billy looked at him, his head on one side.

"Same as the cars?" he asked.

"Same as the cars," Norman said. "You see, they belong to me."

"The cars my Daddy makes belong to you?" Billy questioned, puzzled.

"That's right," Norman said.

Billy thought for some time.

"Then you are Mr. Melton," he said solemnly at length.

"That's right," Norman answered.

"And have you got any boys like me?" Billy inquired.

"I am afraid not," Norman said.

"If you had you could give them all a car for themselves, couldn't you? You wouldn't have to pay for them if they are yours."

"But I haven't got any little boys," Norman said almost sharply.

"Are we going to where you keep all your cars?" Billy asked.

"No, we are not going to the works," Norman said, "you are coming to my house. A big house, where I live."

"I would wather see all the cars," Billy said reflectively.

"So you shall," Norman answered. "I will take you round the works one day, and you shall see them being made."

"And see my Daddy making cars?" Billy asked.

Norman put out his hand and took Billy's small one in his.

"Listen, old boy," he said. "Do you think you could be awfully brave if I tell you something?"

"I'm vewy brave," Billy said, "Mummy says so."

"Your father had an accident this afternoon; he was taken to hospital."

Norman felt Billy's small fingers tighten round his, otherwise the child faced him without quivering.

"Is he hurt?"

"Very badly," Norman said solemnly.

Billy looked at him for a long time, as though considering his next question. Then he asked in a small voice:

"Is Daddy going to heaven like Gwandma?"

"Yes, he has gone to heaven," Norman answered solemnly.

There was a long silence.

"Shan't I ever see Daddy again? Won't I ever get a wide on his bicycle? Never, never?"

"I am afraid not," Norman replied, "but you said you would be a very brave boy. These things happen, you know."

"I would like to have gone on his bicycle again," Billy said forlornly.

"I will give you a bicycle," Norman said impetuously. "I will give you one of your very own. It won't be as big as your daddy's. It will be a small one, of course, but you can ride it."

Billy's eyes brightened, although there was a suspicion of tears in them.

"I can't wide it here," he said. "My Mummy won't even let me have a scooter 'cos there are so many cars in our street I might get wun over."

"You can ride it in my garden," Norman promised. "I will get it tomorrow."

"Will you weally?" Billy said, searching his face for some confirmation of this amazing statement. "You won't forget?"

"I won't forget," Norman promised. "You shall have it tomorrow."

They arrived at the front door of 'The Paddocks'. As usual, the butler and footman were waiting at the open door as the car drew up.

In spite of their long training they could not help registering an expression of surprise as Norman got out, put his arms round a small boy and lifted him on to the ground.

Taking Billy's hand he walked into the hall.

"Where is her ladyship?" he asked.

"She is in the morning-room, Sir Norman. Miss Alice has just left."

Norman opened the door of the morning-room and went in. Carlotta was standing at the window, her hand on the curtain, looking out into the garden. There was an unusually thoughtful expression on her face.

As the door opened she turned round and faced her husband. He advanced towards her. She stared first at him, then at the ragged child he held by the hand.

"Carlotta," Norman said, "I have brought our first guest to stay. His name is Billy."

CHAPTER TWENTY-ONE

Skye ran to shut the windows of the flat as the rain came teeming down, beating against the panes and soaking the net curtains as the gusts of wind blew them to and fro. She stood looking out on to the empty courtyard.

She felt tired and dispirited. This interminable waiting was beginning to tell on her nerves. And it was for Hector that she worried.

She knew that he hated the position into which they had put themselves. Every day that they remained together, with their love unblessed, he felt that he was insulting her.

No amount of argument, nothing she could say, could alter his opinion, which was based firmly on his highest principles.

Although neither of them would have admitted it, the barrier that this raised between them, was beginning in some way to hurt their happiness and injure their love.

It was possible for them not to remember when they kissed and when passion joined them in an ecstasy of happiness, that this frustrated state of affairs might go on for ever.

They were no farther advanced towards being man and wife than they were the first day they had kissed in the shadow of the pine trees.

"I love you," Hector would say. "I love you, Skye."

"I know, darling," she would whisper back.

Yet, because she loved him, she would try to ease, rather than deepen, the tension and the flame between them. She would try to keep the conversation frivolous, to be gay and spirited, rather than emotional and loving.

They had their squabbles too, and although it was but a part of their love, and such differences did not matter in the slightest, the times that they 'kissed and made up' were spoilt.

The evening was drawing on and sooner or later they must go to their own bedrooms, locked away from each other by stronger bonds than any key or chain could devise.

"Shall I write to your grandfather?" Hector once asked suddenly, when he had ostensibly been studying a medical treatise.

Syke looked up from the sewing she was doing and knew that, like herself, he found it difficult to concentrate on anything but the immediate problem of their life together.

"It won't do any good," she answered gently.

"I feel a coward," Hector said. "I ought to have gone to see him. You persuaded me into coming South with you. Now I think I was wrong."

He shut the book with a snap, and got up.

"I ought to talk to him," he said, striding about the room.

"There is nothing you can say that has not already been said," Skye answered. "He's an obstinate old man, but sooner or later I believe he will capitulate. He loves me, in his own way, and he must miss me at Glenholme."

She thought of Glenholme now as she watched by the windows. It had been hot all day before the storm broke, hot and sultry, with that dry, airless atmosphere, so usual in cities when there is a thunderstorm in the air.

Skye felt suffocated. She wanted the freedom of the moors, the wind blowing up from the sea. She wanted more than anything to be in Scotland with Hector.

They both belonged there. They were both happy in uncramped, wild surroundings, far away from struggling, grasping humanity.

'I am ungrateful,' she told herself. 'I have got so much. Hector, his love, and our hopes for the future.'

But she knew that these hopes were beginning to strain during the long waiting.

Supposing, she asked herself, her grandfather would not give in, should she go on, year after year, loving Hector, accepting his love and companionship, able to seek no further union with him?

She knew so surely that if in a moment of madness and lack of control, she could persuade him to become her lover, he would never forgive her or himself.

In spite of his cleverness and his undoubted intelligence, Hector was hidebound. The principles and the religion in which he had been brought up as a child, were still his. He

156

would not lower his standard to circumstances, whatever they might be.

Skye knew that if Hector asked her to, she would go with him to the end of the earth, not caring whether she went as mistress or wife. But he was different. He would not accept a compromise, not even for his own happiness.

The little sitting-room was poorly furnished, for Skye could afford to spend very little money. Her five hundred pounds a year was paid to her only as an allowance, and she could not touch the capital.

Nevertheless, the room was gay and bright. The chintz was colourful with flowers, and the rugs which she had picked up second-hand to cover the floor were in good taste.

"My home," she said aloud, but she knew that it would never be home in truth until she and Hector were married.

For the first time since she had met Hector, Skye felt her courage failing her. She sat down in an arm-chair. Slowly, the tears began to gather in her eyes.

She tried to blink them away, to stop them from falling. They trickled down her cheeks. After a moment she searched for a handkerchief, unable to stop the storm which shook her.

She was startled from her misery by the sound of the electric bell pealing. She jumped to her feet, wiped her eyes, and went towards the door.

'It is only the baker,' she thought.

She gave a pat to her hair and a further rub to her red eyes. She opened the door, and stood startled and surprised. Standing on the doorstep was her grandfather.

They stood regarding each other in silence.

"May I come in?" Lord Brora asked.

"But of course, Grandfather," Skye answered. "I am sorry to be so stupid, but I was so very surprised to see you."

He looked at her from under his eyebrows and she felt that he noticed the traces of tears on her cheeks.

"Come in," she said hastily, leading the way to the sitting-room. "I was just tidying things up. Give me a moment and I will go and powder my nose and look my best for you."

"Don't worry!" her grandfather answered. "I want to see you as you are. Are you alone?"

He looked round the sitting-room as though he expecteed

Hector to pop out from behind a door or from under a chair.

"Quite alone," Skye answered with a faint smile. "Hector is at the hospital."

Lord Brora said nothing. He refused the low arm-chair Skye offered him, and settled himself instead in a high upright one, the type he always found the most comfortable.

"So this is the home you have chosen," he said slowly, looking round.

Skye felt that the bareness of the land was revealed to him.

"We can't afford very much," she explained, "not at present. You see, Hector has only a small amount of money —it was a legacy—and he has put it on one side to keep him until he's through his examinations."

"So McCleod's son is living on your allowance!" her grandfather said sarcastically.

"On the contrary," Skye said. "He gives me all that he can possibly afford towards the housekeeping."

"That's very kind of him," Lord Brora said.

Skye bit her lip.

"I am being quite frank with you, Grandfather," she said, "and I don't want to quarrel, so please don't be rude about Hector. You see, I love him."

"So I imagine," the old man answered.

There was a silence between them.

"Why have you come here?" Skye asked.

"To see you," her grandfather said gruffly.

Skye smiled at him.

"That was very sweet of you," she said, "if you meant it kindly."

"You sent Mary Glenholme up to see me, jabbering about youthful freedom and a lot of tosh," he answered, "and Norman tried to persuade me against his better judgement. I listened to them and I told them what I thought. When they had gone away, I decided to come and see for myself."

"Perhaps you miss me a little?" Skye suggested.

The old man put out his hand.

"Come back to Glenholme, child," he said. "It is lonely there without you."

Skye hesitated for a moment. Then she went towards her grandfather, dropped on her knees beside his chair and looked up into his face.

"Let me come as a married woman," she said coaxingly. "Please, dear Grandfather. You must let me."

The old man started to speak, then choked back the words as they rose to his lips.

"Must!" he said. "What do you mean, must? Tell me, are you . . . ?"

Skye shook her head.

"No, darling," she said. "I am not going to have a baby, it would be easy for me to say I am, because then you would have to give way, wouldn't you? But I will tell you the truth, as I have always told you the truth."

She did not know why, after all her plans, after all the things she had intended to do to force her grandfather's consent, she should throw away her chances at this moment.

She only knew that she could not lie to the old man.

There was something strong, something very fine in him, something which withered all hypocrisy. He might be bigoted, he might be obstinate, but in his own way he was a great gentleman and Skye was proud of him.

She saw the relief which came into his face when she started to speak. She knew it was for this reason that he had come to see her; it was of this that he had been afraid.

She had got to her feet and stood facing him.

"Grandfather," she said, "I have got something to tell you. I never meant to tell you this and I don't know why I am doing it, but somehow I can't help myself. I am living here with Hector under false pretences. It was my idea to live with him and to make you consent to our marriage. He didn't want to do it and he only agreed on one condition."

"What was that?"

"That we should live together only as friends. That there should be nothing between us until we could be married."

When Skye had finished speaking, she turned and walked towards the window. She stood there some moments looking out. Her grandfather knew that she was crying.

"Come here, child," he said gruffly.

She did not obey him and after a moment he repeated:

"Come here, Skye, I want you."

She turned towards him then, and he saw the tears were streaming down her face . . . she advanced a few steps towards him.

Suddenly, she was on her knees beside him, his arms were round her and she was sobbing bitterly against his shoulder.

"I have spoilt it all, now," she said miserably. "I didn't mean to tell you, but I am so miserable, so unhappy, living like this. I want to be married, Grandfather. I want to marry Hector and have a proper home of my own."

He held her tight, one hand round her shoulders, the other stroking her hair. After a time she grew calmer, drawing heaving, sobbing breaths.

Then in a voice rather breathless, she said:

"I have made a fool of myself, haven't I?"

The old man looked down at her with deep affection in his eyes.

"I would like a cup of tea, child," he said, "and you could do with one, too."

Skye tried to laugh.

"Will you have it in the kitchen?" she asked. "Or will you be gentry and stay here until I bring it to you."

"I will have it in the kitchen," Lord Brora replied.

He came with her into the tiny little kitchen. He sat down at the table and watched her cut bread and butter while she waited for the kettle to boil.

"You are looking pale," he said suddenly.

Skye nodded.

"It is lack of Glenholme air and anxiety!" she said with a smile which took the edge off the words.

Her grandfather grunted, then changed the subject.

"Norman gets back from his honeymoon today," he said. "Have you seen his wife?"

"I met her at the station the night he came up to you. She is very pretty."

"And an actress," Lord Brora said, as though that in itself was a complete description.

"Not a very important one," Skye answered. "And I don't think she intends going back to the stage."

"Norman's a damn' fool to marry again at his age," Lord Brora said. "But he seems happy enough, I will say that for him."

"She is not in love with him," Skye said.

"Then why is she marrying him?" the old man asked.

"Money, I suppose!" Skye answered. "Poor Norman, I do hope that he will be happy this time."

Lord Brora looked keenly at his granddaughter, but he let the implication in her last words pass without comment.

He was well aware that Norman's first marriage with his daughter, Evelyn, had not been happy. He seldom discussed such matters, although very little escaped him.

When their tea was finished, Skye put the cups and plates into the sink to wait until she could wash them up.

"How long are you going to stay in London, Grandfather?" she asked.

"It depends on you," Lord Brora replied.

"On me!"

"I thought you would like to come back with me, for a visit, of course."

Skye hesitated. She felt tired and weary of the argument. She felt that she could not go over it all again, yet she did not want to antagonise him by definitely saying no.

She sighed.

Her grandfather took out his large gold hunter watch and looked at it.

"What time does young McCleod get home?" he asked.

"He ought to be here any time now," Skye answered. "I usually expect him about five o'clock."

She waited for her grandfather to get to his feet. Instead he replaced his watch.

"I will see him when he comes," he said.

"You are going to see him!" Skye echoed.

"I will have a talk with him," Lord Brora answered.

Skye waited, half fearful, half defiant.

"I will hear what he's got to say," he added.

Skye gave a little cry.

"Oh, Grandfather! Are you really going to look at things differently? Is there really a chance that you will give your consent?"

"I don't promise anything," was the answer. "I shall just have a talk with this young man, that is all."

Skye flung her arms round his neck.

"You are a darling," she said. "Oh, Grandfather, I never believed you could be so nice about anything."

"Now don't try to harry me," he commanded. "I will make up my own mind and I won't be persuaded by anyone against my own judgment."

She gave him another hug.

"I am so happy," she said confidently. "I know you will love Hector when you see him."

CHAPTER TWENTY-TWO

Carlotta yawned sleepily, stretching her arms as she watched her maid pulling the curtains back from the window to let in the morning sunlight.

"What time is it, Elsie?" she asked.

"It is nine o'clock, my lady," Elsie replied. "I thought you would like to sleep a little later this morning after your long journey."

"I still feel exhausted," Carlotta complained.

Having tidied the room, Elsie went to the door where she was handed a breakfast-tray laden with flowery china and heavy silver dishes.

Carlotta sat up in bed, pushing two lace-edged pillows behind her back.

"I am hungry," she said. "I really think I shall enjoy my breakfast this morning."

"That's right, my lady," Elsie said, "and there's some-one else in the house who has enjoyed a good meal this morning—so cook says."

"Who is that?" Carlotta asked.

"The little boy, my lady. Cook says she has never seen a child eat so much, or enjoy it more. They have been down to the keeper's house to borrow some decent clothes for him and he looks a different child now. You would hardly recognise him. He really is quite handsome now he is properly dressed."

"I will see him when I am up," Carlotta said.

"Sir Norman's very pleased with him," Elsie went on, arranging a set of *crepe de Chine* underclothes on the armchair. "Why, he had him in his room first thing this morning, and they are out now, playing on the lawn. It is a treat to see him. We all think so."

"That will do, Elsie," Carlotta said sharply. "I will ring if I want you."

"Very good, my lady," Elsie said in injured tones, leaving the room with offended dignity.

When she had gone, Carlotta made no attempt to eat the breakfast she had welcomed so gladly. She stared across the room, her forehead wrinkled in a frown, far away from her immediate surroundings.

After a few moments, curiosity overcame her. She pushed back the bedclothes, stepped out of bed in her thin chiffon nightgown and went towards the window.

She approached it stealthily and peeped round the curtains to see a child in a red jersey, careering across the lawn on a small bicycle, with Norman holding him on the saddle and guiding the handle-bars.

"Ridiculous!" she said out loud.

But she did not return to her bed. Instead she stood looking.

Billy was very insecure on his seat and it took all Norman's ingenuity to guide the bicycle and to keep him in place at the same time.

After a few moments they paused. Billy got off and they stood laughing at each other, the sunlight on their faces.

'Norman looks young and happy,' Carlotta thought to herself.

Suddenly she was jealous. Jealous of this child who could take his thoughts away from her, who could wipe away from his expression all the hardness and sternness to which she had grown so accustomed in the past week.

There was something in the flower-filled garden, in the gracious lawns, in the stone terraces, in the house itself with its atmosphere of age and peace, which made Carlotta long more than she had ever done before for security.

She had wanted that when she married Norman, but she flung it away by a few hysterical words, spoken without thought and without consideration for his feelings.

Already she felt as though her coming to 'The Paddocks' was of little importance. She was only a visitor, someone who had come into Norman's life and who was quite likely to leave it again.

On the way back from Cannes she had thought of divorce, but something had stopped her from approaching him about it, from saying to him:

'We have made a mistake. How can we get out of it?'

'I hate him,' she told herself.

But the venom had gone from her voice, as it had gone from her feelings. She no longer wanted to hurt him; she no longer wanted to wound him as she had done yesterday. She felt tired and despondent.

She went back to bed, but all the time she was straining her ears for the faint sound of voices which came through the open window—the deep tones of her husband and the shrill, excited chatter of the child.

Until last night Carlotta had no idea that Norman was fond of children, or that he understood them. She knew that he loved Skye, but she had met her as a grown-up person and had forgotten that when Norman married Evelyn she was only a schoolgirl.

Their conversation had never turned towards children. Carlotta indeed, had thought very little of them.

Vaguely, in the far-distant future, she had imagined that she herself would have a child. But she had thought of such a thing impersonally as being something separate from herself.

So many women that she knew spoke of having a baby as if it were a new car, or another pet to be taken into the household.

Watching Norman with Billy she had seen an entirely different aspect of him.

He was tender; he was gentle with the child; he took trouble to explain things to him; to keep him interested and to prevent him from feeling lonely or afraid in the big house, which was so unlike anything he had known before.

Billy certainly did not lack courage. He considered everything gravely, and with a deep interest. With Carlotta he was a little shy, less talkative than he was with Norman.

"This is my wife, Billy," Norman had explained when he introduced them.

"Is she Mrs. Melton?" Billy asked, addressing himself to Norman.

"That's right, but we usually call her Lady Melton. She likes it," he added with a sly smile at Carlotta.

"Lady Melton!" Billy echoed. "That's pwetty, isn't it, and she is pwetty, isn't she?"

"Very pretty," Norman said briefly.

Carlotta flushed in spite of herself.

Norman had sent the boy into the garden while he explained the circumstances and the tragedy leading to Billy's arrival.

"In the morning Dr. Matthews will take him to the orphanage," he said. "I felt sorry for the poor little beggar, bereft of father and mother in one blow, so I thought I would bring him here."

"Must he go to an orphanage?" Carlotta said. "Surely he must have some relations."

"The doctor is making inquiries," Norman answered, "but I believe they are very happy in the Home. It is a fine place and well run."

"I believe such places are good these days," Carlotta said indifferently.

"He will be homesick, though," Norman added. "It must be like being permanently at school and not being able to look forward to the holidays."

He spoke reflectively. Carlotta looked at him sharply. It was so unlike her impression of Norman's character to be imaginative about such things.

"Can't you get him adopted?" she asked.

"I might," he said.

Without speaking to her further, he went out again into the garden to join the child.

Billy went to bed before dinner and so their first meal together at 'The Paddocks' was a silent one. The dining-room was large and the great mahogany table was laden with silver cups and flower bowls. The butler and two footmen waited on them.

Carlotta found herself overawed by Norman in the surroundings of his home.

At the head of the table he was a far more awe-inspiring person than the man who had whispered attentively to her at restaurants, or in shaded cushioned alcoves in discreet night clubs.

She looked at him with appreciative eyes. He looked nice in his double-breasted dinner jacket, his grey hair brushed back from his high, clever forehead.

After dinner she would have liked to talk with him, but he told her that the agent of the estate was waiting to see him in the library.

"I hope you will find something to do," he said. "There's a wireless in the drawing-room. Ring for somebody to turn it on for you. It is a bit tricky until you are used to it."

"Thank you," Carlotta said.

'This is a cheerful sort of evening,' she told herself angrily as she stood alone in the big empty drawing-room.

She stared at herself in the mirror which hung over the mantelpiece. Her crimson chiffon tea-gown showed up the whiteness of her skin.

She knew she was looking beautiful, a beauty which was entirely wasted on her husband.

'Can love die so quickly?' she asked herself.

It seemed unbelievable, but since that night in Paris nothing she could do or say would make Norman unbend, or show that she held the slightest attraction for him.

She walked towards the window and stood looking out at the summer twilight. It was very still, even the birds had gone to bed. Faintly, in the darkening sky she could see the outline of a new moon.

She turned violently from the window, as though such serenity was more than she could bear. She fumbled with the wireless and got it going.

She turned the tuner until the strains of a swing band echoed and reverberated round the room. . .

When finally she had gone up to her bedroom she had no idea where Norman was or even if he was in the house. She had gone upstairs at half-past nine, after the drinks had been brought in and left on a side table.

"Is there anything you want, my lady?" the butler had asked.

"Nothing, thank you," Carlotta replied.

As he left the room, closing the door gently behind him, she had a wild desire to call him back—to say, "Tell Sir Norman I want him to come here at once."

Only her pride prevented her, only dignity stopped her from going in search of Norman; she was oppressed by a sense of frustration, yet she could do nothing about it.

Now this morning she reviewed, as she had done so many times before, the evening since her marriage day. She had told herself that she would not let Norman win; that she could not let that cool indifference of his continue; that she would break him down; that she would prove herself the victor.

But she was beginning to break first; she was finding the situation intolerable.

She began to see that she was up against something far stronger than herself—a man of great determination, a man whose experience of life had given him weapons she did not possess.

'Soon he will be going to the works,' she thought. 'Without even saying goodbye.'

Ringing the bell hastily she summoned Elsie.

"I want my bath at once," she said.

"But you haven't eaten your breakfast, my lady," Elsie protested, "and you saying you were hungry!"

"I have changed my mind," Carlotta answered. "I want to go out, it is a lovely morning."

"Of course, my lady. I will get your bath immediately."

Carlotta dressed as quickly as she could. She chose a dress of pale-blue linen with sandals to match, beads of carved ivory, which someone had given her as a wedding present, and a white straw hat. When she was ready she ran downstairs.

Norman was in the hall.

"Good morning!" she called out gaily. "Don't tell me you are off to the works, because I want you to show me round the garden."

"I am just leaving," he said.

"Now isn't that disappointing," Carlotta said, "and when were you thinking of coming back?"

"I am afraid I can't get back for lunch today," he answered.

"That's too bad," she said lightly. "It seems that our honeymoon is coming to a very abrupt end!"

At that moment Billy came in from the garden.

"I've got a bicycle," he called out when he saw Carlotta. "A bicycle all of my own. Will you help me wide it?"

"You mustn't be a bother, Billy," Norman said firmly. "Jackson will be coming up later and will help you, but you must play at something else now and not be a nuisance."

Billy ran towards him and slipped his hand into his.

"I will be vewy good," he said. "I pwomise."

Norman looked down at the small eager face looking up into his.

"That's a good boy," he answered. "Dr. Matthews will be coming up to see you later."

"He won't take me away?" Billy asked suddenly.

Carlotta saw his hand tighten on Norman's. There was a moment's silence.

"Don't you want to go yet?" Norman asked slowly.

Billy shook his head.

"I want Mummy," he said. "But I don't want to go away. Can't Mummy come and see me and my bicycle?"

"I am afraid not," Norman answered.

"Please can I stay a little bit longer?" Billy asked, "and play with my bicycle? Please say yes."

"I will talk to Dr. Matthews about it," Norman promised.

He turned to Carlotta.

"I will telephone him when I get to the office. The boy

167

can stay another night at any rate. Will you tell the house-keeper?"

"Of course," Carlotta replied.

"Are you going to see the motor-cars made?" Billy asked.

"Yes," Norman answered.

"Can I come with you?"

"I am afraid not."

"You pwomised I could," Billy said reproachfully.

"If he promised," Carlotta interrupted, "then he must keep his promise. You and I will go to see the cars made this afternoon. We will be there at three o'clock."

She spoke defiantly and Norman knew that she had made this decision merely to annoy him. He accepted her proposal politely.

"I will be waiting for you—both," he said, and went towards the car.

Billy waved good-bye with enthusiasm, but Carlotta stood on the doorstep, watching him go, without making a gesture of farewell.

When the car had disappeared down the drive, she turned towards the house with a sigh.

"Come and see the pond," Billy said to her in an urgent voice. "There are fish in it—wed fish. I've seen them."

Carlotta hesitated, then she let him take her by the hand to the lake where goldfish were swimming amongst the lilies.

"Aren't they pwetty?" Billy said.

"They are called goldfish," Carlotta said to him.

"Are they made of weal gold?"" Billy asked in awed tones.

"Oh, no!" Carlotta laughed. "They are real fish, just like you have for breakfast sometimes."

"They are too pwetty to eat," Billy said decisively, peering down at them.

Carlotta looked at his small sturdy figure in the red jersey that he had borrowed from the keeper's son and his fair hair which glinted in the sunlight.

She thought that by tomorrow he might be taken to the orphanage, to be drilled into the same mould as thousands of other boys, kindly treated, well looked after, but lacking the home life and individual love which every child craves for from a father and mother.

Perhaps Norman had been like this small boy, she

thought. And perhaps Billy would battle his way through the world, even as he had done, and be a great success.

She thought how Magda had looked after her, how she had taken the place of her mother and how she and Leolia had showered love and understanding upon her.

'Poor little Billy,' she thought.

It flashed through her mind that she might take him to Magda and Leolia and ask them to look after him. But they were too old.

They could no longer cope with a child as they had been able to do twenty years ago. They wanted their knitting, their cards, and their cats in peace before the fire.

"Come and show me the rest of the garden," she said to Billy.

She held out her hand.

'I wish he was my son,' she thought.

CHAPTER TWENTY-THREE

The noise of the machinery, the whirl of wheels, the movement and strength of steel, made Carlotta gasp and stand bewildered—a stranger in a new world.

She had never before been round a factory and she had not known exactly what she expected; but certainly something very unlike the truth.

Out of the chaos, the noise and the stupendous unreality of it all, one thing emerged for Carlotta; that was a new aspect of the man who owned it all.

She had never visualised Norman among his own people with the background of his own achievements.

It was not the Norman she had known, courteous and deferential in London, the man who had always seemed slightly ill at ease in restaurants; not the husband who had shown her both authority and an unlooked-for reserve during their brief married life.

This was a man of action; a man on whom great things depended and who had confidence in himself.

Carlotta's vivid imagination could grasp and could understand Norman when she saw him like this, as she had never been able to do when he had appeared to her in her own world—an outsider and an alien.

There was indeed a different set to his shoulders; a different look on his face; and a different manner of speaking.

She watched him in amazement as they walked round the great factory. For the first time in her life she felt small and of no consequence.

Billy was holding tightly on to her hand, but she hardly heeded the child's chatter. It was Norman to whom she was listening.

He said or did nothing unusual, he confined himself to being the polite guide; letting Billy be amused by the smaller machines, speaking sometimes to the minders as he passed, or having a word with the foreman of a department, but every movement that he made, every word that he spoke, was to Carlotta revelation.

As she drove back to 'The Paddocks' in the car with Billy, it seemed to her that a voice inside her was repeating over and over again 'Look what you've missed, look what you've missed.'

The noise of the machinery had told her the same thing; so had the efficiency of the office staff and the shops through which they now passed.

She saw herself as a fool who had proved the old proverb of the shadow and the substance.

She sat in silence until Billy, pulling at her arm, tried to attract her attention.

"Were you fwightened of the big machines?" he asked.

"No, I wasn't frightened," Carlotta answered, "were you?"

"Of course I wasn't!" Billy replied scornfully. "I'm a boy and boys aren't fwightened of anything. But I thought you were a teeny bit fwightened."

Carlotta guessed the child must have felt the trembling of her hand which held his, and in some way sensed that behind the control she kept over herself, was the desire to cry out.

Never before had she realised how difficult it would be ever to destroy the barrier which, by her own careless words, she had erected between Norman and herself.

There, in his own factory, she knew that, apart from the love of a man for a woman, they were poles apart. She saw her own frivolous, useless life—and the conventions which to her had seemed important, the ambitions which were so petty, in their right proportions.

Compared to Norman everything about her was puny and foolish. He was working for reality, she for frivolities which were not worth one moment of the time she wasted on them.

Carlotta was humbled, and because in everything she did she was extreme, she grovelled now among the fallen ruins of her own idols.

"I am tired, Billy," she said.

She tried to excuse herself for not answering a question which she had not even heard.

"When Mummy's tired I'm always vewy quiet," he replied. "I'll be quiet for you now."

She put her arms round him and gave him a hug.

171

"You are very sweet," she said. "I will tell you a story if you like."

He cried out rapturously at the idea and Carlotta racked her brains for a thrilling tale which would wile away the time before they reached home.

At 'The Paddocks' she found a letter waiting for her. She took it up from the oak table in the hall, expecting it to be from Magda or Leolia, but to her surprise it was in a strange writing.

She opened it quickly, looked first at the signature and found it was signed by Honey. It started abruptly and was written in the dashing impetuous manner which was characteristic of Honey herself.

"What do you think has happened? When you get this I shall be on the ocean, heading for the U.S.A. When old Winthorpe—you remember him, don't you —offered me a part in his next film, I nearly fell dead with surprise!

"I have only had four days to collect my clothes together, say good-bye and start off. I have become millionaire-minded, because that's the way I mean to come back! And, Carlotta dear, what do you think? He wanted you too.

"Isn't it too maddening that just as this chance should come, you should have got married and have given us all up. He said:

" 'Where's that girl that used to be here, the peach with the Russian name? I will give her a part as well. She has got the right face for the screen.'

"Of course, I had to tell him who you were and what had happened to you and, my dear, he was absolutely thrilled! I shouldn't be surprised if you hear from him anyway, but of course, there wasn't time to look you up this trip.

"I don't believe you are home, but if you are, send me a cable of good wishes to Hollywood. I shall be thinking of you. Don't forget me in your marble halls, and darling, am I excited! I am! Yours to a cinder,
Honey."

Carlotta read the letter with a smile. She was delighted that Honey should have the chance of making good on the films. She would probably succeed, for she was a good actress, as well as having the type of looks which was always saleable on the screen.

A few weeks ago, Carlotta felt, she too would have been thrilled at the chance of going to Hollywood.

She had been tested for English films and her tests had been good. But the contracts fell through, mostly because the demands they made on her time were unreasonable for the very small salary she would be paid.

'I will send her a cable,' Carlotta decided.

She went to the telephone and picked up the receiver.

When she came back tea was ready, and Billy was waiting with a rapturous expression by the table, staring at a plate of cakes.

"Iced cakes!" he said to Carlotta as she came in. "Is it a pa'ty?"

"Only a very small one," she said, "just you and me. But never mind, there will be all the more to eat, won't there?"

She poured out her tea and gave Billy a cup of milk.

She made an effort to entertain the child, but all the time her mind was wandering, thinking of Norman, of that great factory working day and night, of the motors and of the aeroplanes being turned out ceaselessly.

Quite unexpectedly tears gathered in her eyes and before she could hide them they trickled down her cheeks.

Billy got up from his place at the table.

"Are you hurted?" he asked.

Carlotta shook her head.

"I am just being silly," she said.

He came nearer to her, then impulsively flung his small arms round her neck and pressed his face to hers.

"Don't cwy," he said. "Have you got a pain?"

Carlotta had to smile even through her tears.

"That's it," she said, "I have got a bad pain and I'm not being very brave about it."

"You'll have to take some medicine," Billy said.

"I am afraid no medicine will do me any good," Carlotta replied.

He looked at her very seriously.

"It must be a vewy bad pain," he said.

"It is," Carlotta said with a choking smile. "Finish your tea, Billy, dear. I will go upstairs."

She went out of the room and ran up the broad stairs to her bedroom. When she was there she locked the door.

Wave upon wave of misery was sweeping over her,

breaking down her resistance, and bringing a kind of numb despair. She felt too despondent even for tears.

She seemed to be looking at her heart and seeing within only a misery and a blankness, without a ray of hope to guide or help her.

'What am I to do?' she asked herself.

The confidence she had felt in her own charm and her own beauty to overcome all obstacles, was lost.

Norman appeared to her to be no longer the man who had loved her; the man whom she had once considered of little consequence.

He had, she saw, something that she lacked and something utterly beyond her reach. In comparison he revealed her to herself as cheap and worthless.

'I stabbed him, I wounded him, I deliberately hurt him,' she told herself.

She repeated the words out loud. She walked up and down her room, feeling that the walls confined her as if she were a prisoner without a chance of escape. . .

The impulse came to her to leave at once for London, to see Magda, tell her what had occurred, but a sense of shame made her feel that she could tell no one, not even Magda, how she had behaved to Norman.

The words of her adopted mother on her wedding day came to her mind.

She saw Magda standing in her room after the wedding ceremony. She saw the appeal in her face and heard the pleading tones of her voice.

She had ignored them; she had hardened her heart and deliberately let bitterness and the sense of injustice blind her to everything but her own farcical desire for Hector.

What a fool she had been. What an utter, crazy fool, and this was the result. A marriage that was not a marriage; a husband who despised and hated her—and who could blame him?

After a long time, Carlotta changed her dress, powdered her face and came downstairs. Norman had arrived home from the factory and was playing with Billy.

He had brought him a miniature train and railway lines and they were arranging them in the big drawing room on the parquet floor.

Carlotta stood watching them for a moment from the doorway before they were aware of her presence.

Billy looked up.

"Come and see my pwesent," he exclaimed with a glad shout. "I have got a twain, a wailway twain all of my own."

"And it's a lovely one, too," Carlotta said, coming nearer.

Norman did not look up as she approached. He was kneeling on the floor, fitting the lines into each other. She looked at him, hoping that he would speak to her.

"I enjoyed seeing the factory," Carlotta said at last, almost timidly.

"I am glad," Norman answered, still without looking at her.

"It is rather wonderful to think that you own it," she went on.

"Yes, it is a very paying concern," he answered.

She felt as though he had deliberately slapped her in the face. She checked back the angry words which sprang to her lips and walked away.

From the window-seat she watched Norman arranging the lines so that they went under the piano and round some of the bigger bits of furniture.

Presently he wound up the engine and tried it over the track. He was absorbed in what he was doing, while Billy, with adoration in his eyes, stared at him as though he were something supernatural.

It seemed to Carlotta as though at every turn she found something new in the character of the man she had married and who yet remained to her a stranger.

'Who would have thought,' she asked herself, 'that Norman of all people would have been so clever with children?'

Every day she was learning, but she felt that it was too late, now that an understanding was finally coming to her.

Billy did not go to bed until it was time to go up and dress for dinner. Carlotta came down half an hour later, just as the gong sounded. She and Norman went straight into the dining-room.

They talked a little of conventional things while the servants were in the room, but when finally they were alone and Norman had asked her permission to light a cigar, she asked him a question.

"Did you see Dr. Matthews today?" she said. "What did he say about Billy?"

"I have decided to adopt the child," Norman answered. "He will have to have a governess here in the house until he is old enough to go to school. He's a fine little boy and

I believe that with a decent education and a chance in life, he might develop into a worthwhile man. Anyhow, there's always work for him at the factory."

After a pause he added:

"I shall settle a small amount of money on him to start with, and may increase it further in the years to come."

"I am glad you have decided that," Carlotta said. "He's a darling—he has been extremely well brought up. His parents must have been very nice people."

"I am fond of children," Norman said, pouring himself a glass of brandy, "and as it seems unlikely that I shall have any of my own, I shall have Billy to take their place."

Carlotta clenched her hands together.

"Norman," she said hoarsely, "must you go on like . . . this for . . . ever?"

Norman looked at her and raised his eyebrows.

"Go on like what?" he asked.

"Can't you forgive me?" Carlotta said. "Won't you ever forget what happened the night we were married?"

There was a pause, tense and vibrant.

"How nice of you to ask for my forgiveness," Norman said, slowly choosing his words. "Of course it is yours, if you want it, but I assure you there is nothing to forgive. I like hearing the truth; I prefer it to hypocrisy at any time."

"But it wasn't the truth," Carlotta said. "I swear to you, Norman . . ."

He interrupted her.

"My dear," he said, "you mustn't strain my credulity too far! And why agitate yourself? We have all had a long day, shall we go to the drawing room?"

He rose to his feet and opened the door. Just when she was about to answer him she saw a footman passing through the hall and knew that their conversation would be overheard.

She left the dining-room but she did not go to the drawing-room. Instead she ran upstairs to her bedroom.

"It is hopeless," she said out loud, when she was in the privacy of her own room. "Oh God, how hopeless! And I . . . want him . . . to love . . . me."

She covered her face with her hands, but her eyes were dry. She knew now that there was only one thing for her to do. . .

CHAPTER TWENTY-FOUR

Norman was fast asleep when his valet called him. He hardly stirred as the man pulled back the curtains and carried in a tray of early-morning tea, which he placed by the side of the bed.

Then he picked up the telephone and placed it near his master.

"You are wanted on the telephone, Sir Norman," he said.

Norman half-opened his eyes and yawned.

"What is it?" he asked in a sleepy voice.

"The telephone, Sir Norman," the man repeated.

Norman was instantly awake. The thought of the works sprang to his mind and he sat up in bed, holding the receiver to his ear.

"Hullo, who is it?"

It was Skye's voice that answered him.

"Darling," she said, "I couldn't wait; if you were asleep you will have to forgive me. What do you think has happened?"

"I can't guess," Norman said, "but judging by your voice, I imagine something pretty good."

"It is!" Skye answered. "First of all, Grandfather has consented to our marriage—that, of course, is more important than anything; then Hector has had the most amazing, wonderful offer in the world."

"What is it?" Norman asked.

"He is to go to New York for three years to work in the Rockefeller Institute," Skye answered. "He's not to go for three months, though. We shall be married first. All our expenses are being paid and he will get quite a good salary while he's working there."

"I am glad," Norman ejaculated.

"I'm off my head with excitement," Skye said. "We have turned up trumps at last! It is all so marvellous that I can't believe it is true. Hector only knew very late last night and we were so excited that we went out to dinner. Then it was too late to telephone you; I had to get you as early as I could this morning. We've finished breakfast."

"My dear, I am glad, I really am," Norman said again.

"I knew you would be," Skye went on, "and you were so angelic about Grandfather. He came to see me, I am sure it was all due to you, and he couldn't have been nicer. After he had talked to Hector he realised that we were really serious. Now this has turned up and solves all our problems.

"We shall be away for three years, so that by the time we get back everyone will have forgotten about us, I mean the scandal and all that sort of thing. You do see it is providential, don't you?"

"I certainly do," Norman replied. "And what are you going to do in the meantime?"

"Oh, I have got to go up to Glenholme for a short while. Then can I stay for some weeks at Belgrave Square? I have got to get clothes and all sorts of things; you know what a wedding is like anyway—a million things to see to! May I go to Belgrave Square?"

"You can do anything you like," he promised her.

"Carlotta won't mind, will she?" Skye asked.

"No, she will be delighted," Norman said dryly.

"How is she? Are you frightfully happy, Norman? Hector and I envied you so much on your wedding day that we nearly died of it, and we've thought and talked about you every moment while you have been away."

"That was nice of you," Norman said.

Skye sensed some tension in his voice.

"Everything is all right," she asked, "isn't it?"

"Everything," he replied.

She was obviously not completely reassured.

"I do want you to be happy," she said. "After Hector I love you more than anybody else in the world—you know that!"

"Bless you," Norman said. "And by the way, here is a bit of news that will interest you. I have decided to adopt a small boy."

"Adopt!" Skye said in surprise. "But why?"

Norman told her about Billy and although she said very little, he knew from her questions and from the surprise in her voice that she thought it was a strange thing to do one week after he was married.

178

When finally she rang off, Norman put down the receiver and for some time lay motionless.

He was thinking not so much of Skye's happiness and her good news as of his own life and of the child that he had decided to take under his care.

Norman had thought often of having a child of his own. He had wanted one in the last few years, more than he had wanted anything else, more even than he wanted success. His marriage with Evelyn had been a bitter disappointment.

Although, when he first married her, he had loved her for herself and had given no thought to the family they might have, it was only later as he grew to know and to love Skye, that he wanted a son.

Deep within him there was, in his admiration and his want of Carlotta, the conviction that she was strong, as well as lovely; that she would, in her youth and in her beauty, make the perfect mother for his child.

The hurt she had inflicted upon him on their wedding night was a deeper wound than he would yet admit to himself.

She had shattered not only everything for which he had been yearning these past months since he had known her, but also a castle of dreams that he had built over many years of loneliness and introspection.

Norman had never had a home since his mother died. Life with Alice could never mean the same as life with a mother or a wife.

He had hoped to find in Carlotta the gentleness of his mother in her later years. From the woman whom he loved and who loved him, Norman wanted tenderness as well as passion, maternal understanding as well as the intuition of a lover.

Norman was very humble where the personal side of him was concerned. His marriage with Evelyn had left him uncertain and afraid of women.

Now he saw all Carlotta's advances as lures and wiles to captivate him and hurt him.

He swore to himself that love, for him, had ceased to be. Twice it had failed him and he would never give it a further chance to disturb his life, to bring him unhappiness.

A pride, which until then he had not known he possessed, told him that he must never admit to the outside world that once again he had made a failure of his marriage.

He would put a good face on what was to him a tragedy. He would let no-one know what had occurred and he and Carlotta would live together, ostensibly as a married couple.

'She has married me for money,' he told himself savagely. 'She shall have it. Everything that she wants shall be hers.'

He made plans, the angry plans of a frustrated man who had been hurt and wishes to hurt someone in return. He wrote to Cartier's telling them to have a selection of diamond bracelets ready for him next time he came to London.

He ordered Carlotta a car of her own, the most expensive, super-luxurious that could be obtained. He had paid considerable sums into the bank for her as an allowance.

He took a savage pleasure in doing this and thinking how much he would give to his wife. It was what she had wanted, what she had married him for.

Very well, she should see that he, at any rate, would keep his side of the bargain.

He would plan for Billy also, but in kindness and with forethought for the future which he need not give to Carlotta.

'Perhaps one day,' he said to himself, 'the little chap will take over the factory. I have to leave it to somebody, and God knows who.'

Norman was an idealist. Many years ago he had planned that when Skye grew up she should marry a man who would succeed him when he should die or retire.

Those were dreams that had passed away with many others. But now there was Billy to think of.

His whole scheme was quite clear-cut in his mind. He had a direct way of thinking which made the most complicated problems simple.

He saw no difficulties in the way. The path lay there in front of him. He had only to walk on it.

He tried to erase from his mind all regrets, all memories of those more tender, intimate dreams which had arisen with his love for Carlotta.

'I was a fool,' he thought to himself, 'ever to imagine that such happiness could be mine.'

He saw himself as grim, determined, forceful, not tender or gentle, nor encompassed about by the love of a woman, or the affections of his own children.

He must renounce such things; he must dedicate himself to the future prosperity of his factory, to work for the well-being of the men who served him.

He was glad that Skye would have things the way she wanted them.

He decided that he would write to her at once, and give her as a celebration present the allowance which she had previously refused.

It should be a generous one, for he wanted her to be unhampered by poverty in her new life.

But she was going away from him.

A wave of loneliness swept over him. Once again he seemed confronted with the factory as his only friend— that great grinding impersonal building was the only thing he could lean on and which would lean on him.

He wanted to escape from his thoughts. He sat up in bed and reached for the newspapers which were lying beside him. He turned them over idly.

When the man came he told him to fetch Billy.

"I will talk to him while I am dressing," he said. "Is my bath ready?"

"Quite ready, Sir Norman, and I have put out a blue suit."

"That will do," Norman said.

He got out of bed, sauntered to the window and stood there looking down on the gardens and the park which stretched around the house. It was very peaceful and impressive.

But to Norman it was suddenly unsatisfying, disturbing. It was like old age which was creeping slowly on him, separating him from the world, taking him away from the battlefield of work and vitality.

"There is still so much for me to do." He said the words out loud, almost defiantly.

There was a knock at the door and the valet came in.

"Well?" Norman said abruptly.

"The little boy has gone, Sir Norman," the valet said.

"Gone!" Norman ejaculated. "What do you mean? Gone—where?"

"He left after breakfast," the man replied.

"But where did he go to?" Norman asked angrily.

"Her ladyship took him with her."

"Send her ladyship's maid to me," Norman commanded. manded.

He threw away his cigarette and walked impatiently up

and down the room until Elsie appeared.

Norman saw that she was agitated.

"Where has her ladyship gone to?" he asked.

"I don't know," Elsie answered, trembling. "She told me to pack as many clothes as I could and she left in the car about half-past seven, taking the little boy with her. She was driving herself and she did not tell any of us where she was going."

Norman looked at her for a long time in silence, then he dismissed her.

"That will do, thank you," he said.

CHAPTER TWENTY-FIVE

Norman was dressed in a quarter of an hour. He hurried downstairs and into the library where he rang the bell.

When the butler came he questioned him about Carlotta's movements, only to learn no more than Elsie had already told him.

Carlotta had left the house at half-past seven with Billy and with a great deal of luggage.

She had ordered the car to be brought round and the chauffeur had been waiting for her. But when she came out of the house she dismissed him and drove off herself.

The servants were curious and Norman knew that they were speculating among themselves as to what had happened. He made no attempt at an explanation, or in any way to hide his own surprise at what had occurred.

He merely tried to find from them some clue as to Carlotta's movements, and when they could not help him he dismissed them curtly.

He went upstairs to Carlotta's bedroom. The room was in disorder. Tissue paper was left on the floor, discarded dresses and hats scattered over the bed and chairs.

Elsie was standing among the debris nearly in tears. She was frightened of Norman, and when he came into the room she slipped unobtrusively away, leaving him alone.

He stood for some moments in the centre of the room. It was the first time he had entered it since Carlotta came to the house. There was a faint fragrance in the air of the scent which Carlotta always used.

It reminded him of gardenias, and was reminiscent to him of those evenings when they had driven out together for supper, after she had finished acting at the theatre.

On the dressing table there were one or two scattered objects. A powder-puff, a small box of face powder, an orange-stick.

He picked them up absentmindedly, looking at them as

though they might give him some information as to his wife's whereabouts.

On the writing table there was a pile of papers. He saw that they were bills, some of them unopened, some just stacked together. They were for Carlotta's trousseau, only two or three were receipted.

Lying on the table was a letter. He took it up, looked at the signature. He felt no compunction about reading it. It was from a woman.

A word caught his eye. It was 'Hollywood'.

He read what Honey had written. It seemed to him that here at last was something that might help him. He took the letter in his hand and went downstairs again.

In the library he put through a telephone call to Magda and waited impatiently for the exchange to connect him. He had made it a personal call, and after a few moments the operator spoke.

"Mrs. Lenshovski is unable to take the call, but Mrs. Payne is available, if you would speak to her."

"Put me through," Norman said.

A moment later he heard Leolia's voice, high and agitated.

"Is that you, Norman," she said. "I was just going to telephone you. I am afraid that I have got bad news for Carlotta."

"What is it?" Norman asked.

"Magda had a stroke early this morning," Leolia said. "The doctor has just been and he is sending a nurse. She is still unconscious. We are very anxious."

"I am sorry," Norman said simply.

"She has complained of headaches, of feeling dizzy, lately," Leolia said, "otherwise she has been quite all right. Will you ask Carlotta to come up at once? I think she ought to be here."

"I will tell her," Norman said, "and we will come as soon as possible. Is there anything that you want? Anything that I can do?"

"Nothing, thank you," Leolia answered.

He could tell that she was crying and after a few more expressions of sympathy he rang off.

He did not add to her troubles by saying he had no idea where Carlotta was. He found out what he wanted to know—that she had not gone to Magda.

He picked up *The Times* and looked quickly through the sailing list. He saw, as he had expected to see, that there

184

was a liner leaving Southampton for New York at midday.

Once again he picked up the telephone. He was connected with the works.

"Have an aeroplane ready for me in twenty minutes," he commanded.

There were some difficulties, but he overrode them. Then he sent for the car. While he was waiting for it to come round he drank a cup of coffee, but refused the breakfast which was waiting for him in the dining-room.

The butler hung around, anxious to help, but Norman sent the man away. When he heard the car outside he hurried out, jumped into it.

"As quick as you can," he said to the chauffeur.

They sped down the long drive and along country roads, until they reached the traffic and tramways of Melchester.

Half-an-hour later, Norman, high in the clouds, flying towards Southampton, had time to think. He hoped that his intuition was right and Carlotta was intending to join her friend in Hollywood and take the job which she knew was open for her.

He wondered why she had taken Billy with her.

Then with a sudden illumination, he saw that she was jealous, would not leave him the child to whom he had shown so much attention in the past few days. She wanted to hurt him, to leave him alone with nothing.

Something beside her pride had been disturbed at his attitude towards her. Could she, he asked himself, care for him a little?

Some of the bitterness which had frozen his feelings since the night of his marriage seemed to melt.

He saw Carlotta as a child, torn by her emotions, her temperament unstable and uncontrolled. He saw her defying him, then trying to win back his love and his interest in her.

He saw too, that she had been bewildered, then frightened, when her coquetries had failed, when her looks had been unable to entice him to his knees again.

The world in which she reigned supreme because she was a very lovely woman, had crashed about her. She, too, was alone, but without the reserves that he had, without the experience of having had to walk in loneliness before.

'I am sorry for her,' he told himself; truthfully he added, 'and I love her.'

185

She had wounded him. At the same time he still loved her; still wanted her; still felt, if she would give him the chance, that he could protect her against the world and teach her happiness.

It seemed to him that the plane was moving too slowly. There was an urgency to be with her, to see her again . . .

He checked himself and his thoughts. He had heard Carlotta say that she did not love him, that she had married him for his money.

How could he be so stupid as to go on caring? Why should he ruin his life for a woman to whom he meant nothing?

He tried to think of other things, to remember only that he was hurrying to tell the wife who did not care for him that her adopted mother was dangerously ill.

But in spite of himself and his common sense, his pursuit of Carlotta was a crusade for his own happiness. For the last time he was fighting for her affection. If he was defeated now, it would be the end . . .

He wondered what Carlotta had said to Billy. In some ridiculous manner he was glad that the child was with her. She would be more careful of herself, she would be less reckless with the boy by her side.

She had three hours' start and more than once he took out his watch and wondered if he would be too late. The wind was against them, retarding their progress.

Nevertheless, the aeroplane boomed steadily on, lurching every now and again, passing through various bumpy patches as they headed south.

It was nearly eleven o'clock when finally they reached the airport at Southampton. A car was waiting for Norman. He had told his secretary to telephone and arrange for one to be in readiness.

"The docks!" he commanded.

It took them some time to get through the narrow crowded streets of Southampton down to the docks. Passengers were climbing aboard the great liner, luggage was being swung into the hold.

There was the usual feverish activity which accompanies every departure of a great ship.

Norman went to the purser's office and made inquiries. He wondered whether Carlotta would travel under her own name or under his. After some delay he was told the number of her state-room. He went to it.

186

He knocked. For a moment there was no answer. Then a quiet voice said:

"Come in."

He opened the door. Carlotta was sitting on the bed in a listless, despondent attitude. Billy was playing happily on the floor with a mechanical toy.

It was he who saw Norman first. He got up with a shout of welcome and ran towards him.

"I'm going on this big ship," he said, "to America."

Carlotta looked up. Her eyes met Norman's.

"Why are you going away?" he asked.

He spoke very gravely and quietly.

Without choosing her words, she answered him truthfully.

"Because . . . I am . . . so . . . terribly . . . unhappy."

"I am sorry," Norman said, "very sorry, Carlotta."

She turned her face away from him.

"It is too late . . . now. You won't . . . forgive me. I can't go on . . . any more. It is hopeless . . . quite . . . hopeless."

Norman walked across to her and put his hand on her shoulder. She started a little at his touch and then was very still.

"Carlotta," he said, "you have got to come back to London, now, at once. It is Magda. She is ill."

Carlotta gave a little quivering cry, like an animal that has been hurt.

"Magda ill!" she said. "What has happened? Tell me quickly!"

Norman reached out for her hand and took it in his own.

"She has had a slight stroke," he said. "Leolia Payne rang me this morning. She wants you to come at once."

Carlotta was very white. She got to her feet, picked up her bag and her coat which lay beside her.

"I must . . . go . . ." she said unsteadily. "Will you . . . take me?"

Norman rang the bell. When the steward came he gave instructions about the luggage. Then, holding Billy by the hand, he followed Carlotta down the passages towards the gangway.

They stepped ashore into the bright sunlight. After a short wait the luggage was brought off and piled up on the car.

As they drove off Carlotta turned towards Norman sitting at her side, and spoke for the first time since they had left the cabin.

"Shall we be too . . . late?" she asked.

"I hope not," he said.

She was trembling and he saw that her eyes were filling with tears. She opened her bag, searching blindly in it for a handkerchief. He took the one from his pocket and gave it to her.

"If only I had gone to . . . see her," Carlotta said in a low voice. "Why didn't I . . . instead of coming . . . here?"

"We shall be there in two hours," he said comfortingly.

"Magda . . . my beloved Magda," Carlotta whispered beneath her breath.

As if she could control herself no longer, a tempest of weeping shook her. She buried her face in her hands.

Instinctively Norman put out his arms and drew her close to him. She made no effort to resist him, letting her head drop on his shoulder.

"If she dies," Carlotta sobbed, "that is the . . . end. I shall be . . . left! Alone with . . . nobody to . . . care for me."

"My dear," Norman murmured. "That is not true."

"It is true! It is true." Carlotta answered wildly. "She loved me. She was the only person. I have been so miserable . . . so un . . . happy. Oh, Norman, why do you . . . hate me?"

He could hardly hear her words, for her face was buried against his shoulder.

Her unhappiness affected Billy. He whimpered and left the small seat on which he had been sitting to move close to Norman. He was tired after his long drive, frightened by Carlotta's misery.

Norman put his other arm round the child. Billy leant confidently against him.

As if she felt his attention wander from her, Carlotta drew closer.

"Take care of me . . . Norman. I can't . . . bear it."

The words were wrung from her.

"I didn't . . . understand . . . but I . . . love . . . you . . . I do . . only you won't ever . . . believe . . . me."

She sobbed despairingly.

"I only thought . . . I . . . loved Hector . . . because he . . . didn't want . . . me."

Norman stiffened in surprise.

"And I . . . thought I only . . . wanted . . . your money,"

188

Carlotta wept, "but I . . . was such . . . a fool . . . I loathe your money . . . I want you . . . you . . . you . . ."

Her voice became incoherent and she collapsed completely. Her whole body shaken by her agonising weeping.

Billy was crying too.

Norman looked down on their two heads and a strange expression softened the gravity of his face.

He realised that this moment was the beginning of his family life.

"It is all right, my darling," he said quietly. "It is all right."